jill marshall moved from the United Kingdom to New Zealand, along with her small daughter and her even smaller mad dog. Her childhood ambition was to become an author, so in 2001 Jill gave up her career at a huge international company to concentrate on writing for children. When not working, writing and being a mum, Jill plays guitar, takes singing lessons and is learning to play the drum kit she has set up in the garage. One day she might even sing in a band again . . .

Look out for the seventh book in the
jane blonde series:

**jane blonde, spylets
are forever**

Also by Jill Marshall

jane blonde, sensational spylet★
jane blonde spies trouble
jane blonde, twice the spylet
jane blonde, the perfect spylet
(for world book day)
jane blonde, spylet on ice
jane blonde, goldenspy

Look out for

jane blonde, spylets are forever

★*also available in audio*

Jane Blonde

spy in the sky

JILL MARSHALL

MACMILLAN CHILDREN'S BOOKS

First published 2008 by Macmillan Children's Books
a division of Macmillan Publishers Limited
20 New Wharf Road, London N1 9RR
Basingstoke and Oxford
www.panmacmillan.com

Associated companies throughout the world

ISBN 978-0-330-45812-2

1 3 5 7 9 8 6 4 2

A CIP catalogue record for this book is available from
the British Library.

Typeset by Nigel Hazle
Printed and bound in the UK by CPI Mackays, Chatham ME5 8TD

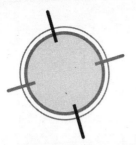

this book was written 'on the cusp', as it were, so thanks and thanks again for seamless transitions to: rachel and emma for sorting out my authorly vagueness with such insight and general loveliness; angie and jane for girls' nights out and so much more, dom for being the very best of both parts of the world, and talya for global corrections and remembering way more than i do. what olympian tag teams – you are a pleasure to work with! to glenys, for superb international communications and being there, wherever 'there' happens to be, thank you as always. to karren and the michael king writers centre, thanks for putting up with my coming-and-goings; i couldn't have written this book without the peace and respite the centre offers (and coffee and chats in the kitchen). to mum and dad and katie, for the same and so much besides, with lots of love. and to agent morning and all those other ace spylets out there, your spy messages are an inspiration. keep 'em coming!

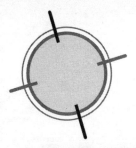

for my talented and brilliant nephews and nieces:
richard, nick, emma, dom, christopher, hollie,
jack and larissa xxx

contents

dark dreams

'No! No, you mustn't . . . Please!'

Janey Brown sat bolt upright and glanced at the clock. Ten o'clock. It wasn't that long since she'd gone to bed, but these days it wasn't unusual that she'd fallen so quickly into such a deep sleep. She'd been having some funny dreams lately too, since she'd been zapped in the stomach with Copernicus's supersonic Lay-Z Beam a couple of months before. It was only thanks to her golden SPIsuit that it hadn't blasted a hole straight through the middle of her. But her peculiar nightmares had never woken her up before. Had it been her own voice calling out?

No. There it was again. A man's voice. Her dad's voice, to be more precise. Boz Brilliance Brown, also known as Abe Rownigan, and sometimes Solomon Brown, was shouting next door. 'No, stop it. Let me . . . No!'

He was in G-Mamma's Spylab. Janey's heart turned over. Perhaps, if they were lucky, he was sleep-walking and imagining things.

1

But if they weren't so lucky . . .

Who could his attacker be? Their arch-enemy, Copernicus, was currently suspended in a glass case in the NASA centre in Florida, trapped in his vile half-squid body.

'I . . . fight . . . not the revolver . . .'

Her father's frantic cries came through to her in jagged sound bites. But one word flung her into action: *revolver*.

Someone was going to shoot him.

Aware that she was only in her pyjamas, and that the route to the Wower, where she could transform into Sensational Spylet Jane Blonde, might be blocked, Janey grabbed the nearest heavy item – her clock. She smacked the wall above her fireplace at the ten-past-two position to activate the panel at the back that led to the Spylab and crouched down, ready to spring forward.

With agonizing slowness the iron plate separating the two rooms edged upwards, and the scuffling beyond grew louder, more furious. Janey could just make out her father's legs, bent at an odd angle as if he was in a tug of war, pulling something heavy.

'Please . . . I can help!' he was shouting, his voice anguished. Janey had never heard him sound so . . . so desperate. Almost begging. What must that creature be doing to make him sound like that?

'Come on,' urged Janey as the panel finally slid up and the tunnel through to G-Mamma's fireplace opened up fully. She drove herself forward on her elbows, desperate to get in there before the revolver had a chance to go off. She was almost through now. Almost able to see what hideous enemy her father was struggling with. She could make out a pair of legs. Feet. Small. Smaller than hers. One of her old enemies returned, maybe? It could be Freddie/Freda, or Paulette – they were both tiny. And Freda had been very fond of her little bronze gun.

But it was hard to figure out anything more in the whirl of wind that was flinging papers and small SPI-buy gadgets across the Spylab, plastering her father's trousers to his legs, as he leaned . . . reached . . . grabbed for something . . .

'Dad!' Janey scrambled forward, trying to shield her eyes from the strange light, a glaze of midnight blue that seemed somehow to be all darkness and all brightness at the same time. She wished desperately for her Ultra-gogs, which would have given her a clear view of what was going on, a chance to attack the gun-wielding monster at large in the Spylab.

'Dad, I'm here!'

Her mousy hair was plucked from her shoulders, lashing her face from all sides. The mysterious glow was pulsating, that strange combination of dark and light. She couldn't make anything out, but she raised the clock above her head in what she hoped was the direction of the enemy. 'Dad . . . let me . . .'

But then the whistling wind, swirling around like the vortex from her SPIroscope, twitched the clock from her hands. It clattered on to the tiled hearth and she saw – or rather felt – her father spin around to see her.

'Janey! No! Get back, I can handle this. Get . . . I . . . it . . .'

For a few seconds he was there in front of her and then he disappeared out of view, off to the left. Then he was back again. And gone. Again and again. Brief glimpses of his face. Pained. Terrified.

But just as she managed to reach out a hand to grab a desk lamp she spied someone shrinking back into the corner. Now. She should throw the lamp at the attacker now. But there was her dad again. She might hurt him. Gone. Back again. Gone. Back again.

And suddenly the decision was taken out of her hands – literally. With a brutal twitch, the spinning wind took hold of the lamp and flung it into the centre of the Spylab. It split the cylinder of light that Janey could now see more clearly as the lamp disappeared inside it. There was a cry . . . two cries . . . and then a hundred things happening at once . . .

With a stomach-churning ripping noise something substantial pounded across the Spylab floor and flew out through the open window. Her father screamed and then slumped to the floor; the SPIral staircase creaked as someone leaped on to the top step and raced downstairs, through the door and out; the peculiar column of sickly black light made a furious zipping noise, stretched towards the window, blowing out all the screens in the computer banks along the work-bench and the wall, and then folded in on itself until it disappeared in one last tiny pinprick of concentrated darkness.

'Dad?' Janey raced over to her father's prone body. He looked dazed and a bit green around the edges, as if he'd just got off a fairground ride. 'Are you OK? What was that?'

She took his hand as he propped himself up on one elbow. 'What was what?' he said slowly, when he finally looked sure that he wasn't going to be sick.

'That weird light and dark thing. Was that . . . was that an enemy?' It had not looked like something of this world. And Janey would put nothing past Copernicus and his team of evil spies.

'It's nothing,' said Boz, rubbing her fingers with his thumb. 'Nothing for you to worry about.'

'But there was someone here! Someone with a gun. I heard you say,' said Janey. 'That wasn't nothing.'

Her father sat up and tousled her hair. 'Go back to bed, Janey,' he said, easing himself into a standing position and pulling Janey to her feet. 'There's noth-ing to worry about.'

'I am a bit . . .' Janey smothered an enormous yawn '. . . a bit sleepy, now you mention it.'

5

Her father nodded, his expression one of great fondness tinged with a tiny hint of . . . of what? Janey couldn't quite work it out. Sadness, maybe? Regret? She shrugged. No idea. Her head felt rather woolly.

'Did you have a dream, Janey? You've been having them a lot lately.'

She wasn't sure. 'I thought . . . Oh, I don't know. I have been dreaming some funny things.'

And Janey's father dropped a kiss on to her fore-head and pushed her gently towards the fireplace tunnel. 'A good sleep will make you feel better.'

'Yes,' said Janey. 'A good sleep.'

She clambered back through the tunnel and into bed, wondering at how wild her imagination had become. That Copernicus had a lot to answer for . . . Good job she was a Sensational Spylet, with SPI – her father's international spy organization – behind her, she thought. And then she fell sound asleep.

the name game

The summons to the naming ceremony came at two o'clock that morning. G-Mamma had squeezed her way through the fireplace tunnel between her Spylab and Janey's bedroom and was looming over the bed like Mummy Christmas, in her scarlet and white SPIsuit, complete with floppy hat.

'Come on, Blonde,' she barked, sergeant-major-like. 'Important stuff going on next door.'

Janey sat up abruptly. 'Am I dreaming again?'

G-Mamma grabbed Janey's arm between two talons and pinched hard. 'Did that hurt?' she purred innocently as Janey cried out. 'Then you're awake, Janey baby.'

'Ow,' grumbled Janey, rubbing her arm as she swung her long legs out of the bed. 'So what's going on? I just had this weird . . . dream. It was all tall and black and dark and light, all at the same time. With a gun! Yuck.'

'Too much cheese before bed?' suggested G-Mamma. 'This is nothing like that.'

'Well, what then?'

'You'll see with your spying eyes,' was all G-Mamma would say, before she dropped to her knees and squirmed her way back through to her Spylab next door.

Janey pulled on her dressing gown, brushing away the little square of clear plastic that was lodged in her hair. A sweet wrapper, no doubt, courtesy of G-Mamma. She followed, only to find that when she stood up at the other end of the tunnel, the room she was in was no longer her SPI:KE's Spylab. In the corner where G-Mamma's make-up bench had stood there was now a large bed, and next to it an expanse of desk covered in maps, architectural drawings and all sorts of doodles and scribbles in her father's handwriting. Maybe that was what her nightmare was about – she'd heard the removals going on in here and her overactive brain had incorporated the noise into her dream.

Lined up along the edge of the bed were her father, her mother (even after a few weeks it still amazed her that the quiet, unassuming Jean had finally uncovered her own identity as Gina Bellarina, super-SPI) and the newest member of the family, James, in shorts and a T-shirt. Her friends Alfie Halliday and his mum were leaning on a nearby computer bench, Wowed up in their finest SPIsuits, and loitering near the SPIral

8

staircase were two more spies: Spylet Titian Ambition and her mother, Magenta, glowing in their matching red Lycra suits. Everyone looked solemn, but not in the usual SPI way that meant some dire disaster was about to befall the universe. More like people going into church, thought Janey.

She was the only one in pyjamas. G-Mamma gestured towards the shower cubicle with her eyebrows and, stepping in, Janey instructed the Wower to work its magic. In mere moments she emerged in her stretchy silver SPIsuit, hair tumbling bright and blonde from a topknot, and her grey eyes framed by slender Ultra-gogs.

'We're all ready then,' said Boz. 'We let you sleep in a bit, Janey, after . . .'

'. . . after I zapped myself in the stomach with a world-numbing Lay-Z Beam,' finished Janey. 'But I'm really much better now, apart from the odd nightmare. Right back to normal.'

She looked over at her new little brother, whose gloomy dark eyes featured a lot in those dreams. They were brighter now, of course, now he'd found a family who cared for him, but still tinged with a certain sadness. Janey felt like rushing over to give him a hug, but Gina was taking his hand, and together they walked towards the middle of the room.

Boz waved his hands to draw the SPIs in around him, and Janey linked arms with Magenta and G-Mamma, surprised at the seriousness of her father's expression. 'We're welcoming a new member to our team,' said Boz quietly, gazing straight into James's furrowed little face.

'Yes, we thought we'd do something special for James,' said Janey's mum, smoothing down her bronze Lycra suit self-consciously. 'He's a special boy, after all.'

'No kidding,' muttered Alfie, round to Janey's left, and his mother gave him a shove. Rolling his eyes, he motioned that he was buttoning his lip.

But it was the truth, after all. Until James had come into contact with the Rapid Evolution process, he hadn't been a boy at all. He'd been quite happy sitting in a cage, conversing in sign language with the other chimps, especially his sister, Belle.

Boz laid his hand on James's head. 'James, we want you to know that you are part of our family, and part of our team. You are a SPI Spylet now, and we would like to give you your Spylet name and Spylet identity.'

'Do you have to wet his head like a baby's at a christening?' blurted Tish, direct as ever.

'Sort of,' said Boz with a grin. 'Only we'll do it in the Wower.'

And with that the circle of SPIs opened, forming a corridor. Boz led James over to the spy shower, the mirrored exterior reflecting Boz's solemn, handsome face alongside James's slightly bowed figure. He walked along quietly until Boz reached over to open the door, but then suddenly he started to struggle.

'Dad, he's frightened,' called Janey. 'Last time he went in a machine he got changed into a whole different species, not just a new SPIsuit.'

'Oh, of course,' said Boz, loosening his grip on James's hand. The boy pulled free and ran over to Janey.

'It's all right,' said Janey softly, smoothing down his hair. 'Look, I just went through the Wower, and I'm still me, just in a SPIsuit. It won't hurt.' She held up her little finger. 'Pinky promise.'

James watched her for a moment, then raised his pinky to link with hers. It was how they communicated – with gestures and sign language – since James could understand English but couldn't speak it. They both pulled once, twice, sealing the promise, then Janey pushed him gently towards the Wower. With one backward glance in her direction, James took a deep breath and stepped inside. 'Wow him,' Janey ordered the machine as the door closed.

It only took a minute, or maybe less, before she heard a tapping at the Wower door. She pulled it open, and out stepped a confident young man with his shoulders back, smiling broadly. He wore a brilliant white SPIsuit with black slashes across the legs and arms, rather like zebra stripes, and black-rimmed Ultra-gogs the same colour as his glittering eyes and hair. James looked around a little shyly, then stuck both thumbs up in front of him and grinned.

'You like that then?' Janey laughed. 'You look great.'

Boz smiled. 'SPIs and Spylets, I introduce our newest member: Spylet Jimmy Sable.'

'Sable the able!' yelled G-Mamma, thinking up a rap on the spot. 'Oh yes indeedy! Able and sable, that's our boy, and with us he'll have loads of joy . . .'

Tish looked confused. 'What does "sable" mean?'

'Black, like his hair,' Alfie told her. How he knew that, Janey couldn't imagine – but then she noticed that he'd whipped off his PERSPIRE hat and looked it up on the mini-computer in its crown. Alfie really liked to be the first to know things.

Jimmy Sable looked down at his suit as proudly as Janey had the first time she had transformed into Jane Blonde. She held her hand out to him and he shook it solemnly. 'Welcome, Spylet Sable,' she said.

And then everyone took his hand in turn, making him feel special, making sure he felt wanted. His smile became even bigger when Janey's mum turned around with an enormous cake lit with candles that looked like tiny sticks of SPInamite, and everyone in the room applauded.

After that it was just like a birthday party. Or at least, she imagined it was. She hadn't been to many. Janey chatted to Tish, played computer games with

Alfie and ate handfuls of cake, once she'd managed to distract G-Mamma from it with a toss-the-jelly-bean-into-your-mouth competition. G-Mamma won easily, then complained that the sugar was hurting her teeth.

All too soon, the party was over. Slivers of pink light were peeking through the blinds. Morning.

'Time to de-Wow, I think,' said Boz with a yawn.

'I'll go last, seeing as my bedroom's closest,' offered Janey, but her father pointed to the bed in the corner.

'I'm taking this room, and James will sleep downstairs,' he said. 'That way you and your mum can still have your space next door without us boys getting in the way.'

Janey stared at him. 'What about G-Mamma? And where's all her stuff gone anyway?'

'I've been rehoused.' G-Mamma managed to sound only a tiny bit frosty, but Janey could tell that she wasn't happy about it.

'It's only temporary,' said Boz quickly. 'G-Mamma's got a new Spylab in the garage at the bottom of the garden.'

'So actually, G-Mamma,' said Alfie, snickering, 'you've been re-shedded.'

G-Mamma smiled brightly, making the best of things. 'All the latest gadgetry, in my own little granny flat. I mean, erk, in my G-Mammy flat. It's lovely. Drop by,' she finished with a toss of her pink-tipped blonde curls, before flouncing off down the SPIral staircase.

Hmm, thought Janey. Her father and new Spylet brother living next door. Her mother desperate to start spying again after so many years. And G-Mamma 'rehoused' in the garden.

It was going to be a very interesting summer.

3 pelicans and pilots

So this is what it's like for everyone else, thought Janey a couple of weeks later. She propped her head up on her hand as she tipped milk on to her cornflakes. Opposite sat her father, hunched over the newspaper, which he flicked through with one hand while feeding himself boiled egg with the other. Badly. At least Janey's mother, scraping the cremated crumbs off her toast, added some colour to the scene: she was wearing her bronze SPIsuit, as she'd insisted on doing every morning since she'd rediscovered her spy identity. She'd even gone to her cleaning jobs in it, with the gleaming Lycra cleverly hidden under a long overall and rubber gloves.

James nudged Janey's arm, and she followed his long finger to see what he wanted. 'Yoghurt? Oh, sugar.'

She helped James sprinkle sugar on his chopped banana. Fruit was still his favourite food, despite everything G-Mamma had done to introduce him to doughnuts, burgers and fried peanut-butter sand-wiches. He'd licked the sugar off the doughnuts and scraped the peanut butter off the bread with a finger, but everything else had been spat on to the floor with a look of disgust.

Janey sighed, watching him prod a piece of banana with his fork. So much for thinking it might be an interesting summer. The weeks had stretched on and on, milk-white mornings fading to late summer bed-times, without a mission in sight. Even with her father close by, right in the firing zone, there was nothing to do. Since the naming ceremony, the highlight of the summer had been teaching James how to play football (or rather trying to join in while Alfie taught James how to play football) and getting uniform items for her new school from Seacrest and Argents department store.

Even the bad dreams had stopped completely. She hated Copernicus. She really did. But with NASA scientists checking his every breath and brainwave pattern, he was safely out of the way – and life was extremely dull.

'What are we doing today?' she said eventually, when the sound of everyone chewing and slurping had finally got to her.

The newspaper opposite her folded down. 'I'm still on holiday,' said her father with a grin that took in James as well. 'I'm doing nothing.'

'Me too,' said Jean Brown. 'We can do nothing together.'

They gave each other such a soppy look that Janey felt a bit nauseous. She'd wanted so much for her dad to be around, and for her mum to realize this man was actually her presumed-dead husband. But now that they were reunited it made her feel extremely uncomfortable to see them kissing, or twinkling their eyes at each other in some weird, adults-only way.

'What about you, Jamie?'

James looked up and twiddled his right-hand fingers across his left palm.

'Football? OK.' It was better than nothing.

But James shook his head and repeated the action, more slowly this time.

'Just for a walk then. That's fine. I'll get my hat . . . no?' James was shaking his head again, pointing at his chest. There was no mistaking what he meant. 'Oh. You want to go on your own.'

James nodded.

'You're too little,' said Janey, just a little petulantly. She hadn't been allowed to go off on her own until the last couple of months (apart from at night, on her missions, when her mother had known nothing about it), and James was much younger than she was.

Gathering the breakfast dishes, Jean Brown shot Janey a warning glance. 'Janey, James can look

17

after himself. He has been through an awful lot without anyone holding his hand.'

Janey was about to protest that she'd been through quite a lot herself, when she noticed her mother wiggling her eyebrows and sending meaningful looks at the newspaper. A large advert for Solfari Lands, the zoo belonging to her father, which acted as yet another cover for his spy activities, rippled across the front page. 'MEET THE CHIMPS,' it declared. 'ENCOUNTERS AT 10.30 A.M. AND EVERY HOUR UNTIL CLOSING.' Now she understood. James wanted to see his sister. His *other* sister, she corrected herself. His *chimpanzee* sister.

So that was that. Her mum and dad had each other. James preferred his other sister to Janey. And she had nothing to do. 'I'm going to see G-Mamma,' she huffed.

The building where G-Mamma now lived and worked still looked exactly like a garage. Its gravel driveway ran between rows of houses on one side and allotments – where some organic turkeys were being bred – on the other. The allotment turkeys' devotion to G-Mamma and her never-ending supply of leftovers was positively slavish, and they scurried to the fence, eyes bulging, whenever she appeared.

The whole place had a ramshackle, disowned air about it, and the main entrance was through a rotting wooden door that opened directly on to the garden. Inside, however, G-Mamma had transported the place into the twenty-second century. The space under the roof that had previously been used to store old tents and cricket sets had somehow been opened up to provide a sleeping platform dripping with fairy lights and candelabra, which Trouble, Spycat extraordinaire, had adopted as his personal throne area. Access was by way of a chrome SPIral staircase, which G-Mamma could also use to burrow through the earth to Australia at the drop of a large, flowery hat.

'Blonde! Nice of you to call by.' G-Mamma waved.

The double garage doors had been covered in mirrored glass; one half housed the sleekest of refrigerators, and the other opened up to display G-Mamma's cosmetics collection in its full glory. All along the side walls were immense white filing cabinets, switch-activated to rotate far into the earth, so that despite the small size of the garage, the SPI:KE could still accommodate a full range of SPI-buys and a complete bank of computers, sound synthesizers and technological equipment. In place of her usual benches, G-Mamma had a folding Workmate in gleaming platinum and a shiny plastic bar stool on wheels, on which she sailed around the garage like a chubby heron.

Only a fat old tractor tyre in one corner, now

spray-painted white and daubed with pink and yellow daisies, gave any indication of the building's original purpose. Trouble had taken to dropping half-dead birds into the tyre's hole, and he added the latest to his collection as Janey watched in disgust. Animals, she thought. Sometimes you couldn't stop them being – well, animals.

'So what's going on in Brown Towers?' G-Mamma tried to twinkle at Janey in her usual eye-glittering way, but it wasn't working. 'New mission? Don't know how I'd cope. I'm *soooo* busy.'

'Nothing's going on,' said Janey. 'And you're as bored as I am.'

'Me? Bored? Me?' G-Mamma waggled her outfit-matching pink fingers at Janey. 'Never! I've got my SPI:KE-y hands full this very moment.'

'With what?' Janey asked eagerly. 'Maybe I could help.'

'Well, today,' said G-Mamma, reaching into her Workmate and fumbling around, 'I have invented SParrows. The world's first SPI arrows. They're going to be as indispensable as SPInamite, or your trusty Girl-gauntlet.'

She held one up for Janey to see. A thick wooden pole had been roughly sharpened at one end, with flights made from pink feathers attached at the other. G-Mamma waved it around like a wand and threw back her head in preparation for a major rap.

'Sparrow power, it's here, it's here,
Sparrow power; feel the fear, feel the fear . . .
They fly through the air like birds on the wing,
Get out of their way or you'll feel their sting.
Sparrow power, it's here, it's here.
Feel it, squeal it, FEEL THE FEAR!

'Do you know, I really should go into advertising – if I ever find myself in need of a job.' She gave Janey a tight smile.

'Um, G-Mamma,' said Janey gently, handing back the missile, 'it's a cricket stump with feathers on it.'

G-Mamma leaped off her chair. 'Well, it is *now*, my doubting Spyletti, but wait till it's been Wowed!'

Janey smiled. 'I see. Although hang on a second – where *is* your Wower?'

'In a space as terribly teensy as this, I mean, as *cosy* as this, everything has to have two purposes,' said G-Mamma. She tapped out a rhythm on the bottom step of the SPIral staircase and, sure enough, it swivelled around to reveal a narrow cylindrical spy shower. Opening the door, G-Mamma called, 'Wow the Sparrow,' as she lobbed the feathery cricket stump inside

Janey fiddled with the TV remote controls as she waited. Suddenly the left-hand mirrored door went misty, and the voice of a newscaster droned out into the room. 'Gosh, everything does have two uses,' she said, trying to change the channel. Nothing happened, and the newsreader's voice boomed out as an image flickered into life on the fridge – a picture of a small jet plane, its nose mangled out of shape, with two sheepish-looking RAF officers pointing to it.

'And finally,' said the newsreader, 'a fighter jet on a training mission in Scotland had to make an emergency landing when an enormous bird struck the fibreglass nose and was almost sucked into the engine. The brand-new Joint Combat Aircraft was flying at nine hundred metres when the bird, thought possibly to have been a huge pelican caught way off course, zoomed into their sights and struck the plane. The RAF has admitted that the plane was flying over built-up areas, including the Sol's Lols ice-lolly factory, and it is only thanks to the skill of the pilots that the damaged jet did not crash-land, causing many fatalities. The pelican is missing, presumed dead.'

'Look!' screeched G-Mamma, brandishing something in Janey's face. 'It's brilliant. Look at that!'

Janey stared at her, open-mouthed. 'Didn't you hear that? Sol's Lols has—'

'I've invented a SPI-buy. A few little adjustments . . . I'll. Be. RICH!' And at that G-Mamma danced around the garage, holding the cricket stump above her head as if she'd just won the Olympics with it.

'G-Mamma, something's wrong,' Janey shouted, grappling for the SParrow. 'Some fighter jets were flying over Sol's Lols! Don't you think that's fishy? Maybe someone was trying to attack the Spylab.'

G-Mamma sat down with a *whump*. 'Bumpy bombers . . . show me!'

The news item had finished. Janey flicked through the channels, but nobody was covering that item. 'It was a plane. The RAF, they said. Can't we at least look it up?'

'OK,' said G-Mamma with gusto. She pulled up the computer panels and tapped into the keyboard. The latest news scrolled down the page. 'Well, it mentions the pelican and the pilots' malarkey, but nothing about Sol's Lols. Maybe it's just coincidence.'

'Well, they wouldn't need to mention it, would they, if it hadn't actually been hit? That big bird probably stopped them before they had the chance to bomb the building.'

'Or maybe, baby Blondey, you are so bored and dying for some little mission to zip off on, you're just letting your imagination run away with you.' G-Mamma cocked her head, fluttering her eyelashes so fast that Janey giggled.

'Maybe, but I'm still not convinced. The whole thing's weird. And pelicans are sort of tropical, aren't they? Not the kind of the thing you usually find flying around Scotland,' she said eventually. 'I'd better leave you to invent the bow for your cricket stump. I've a feeling we might need it.'

'The bow? Oh, the firing thingy. Yes, oh yessy.
I'll be like Robin Hood.' The SPI:KE's eyes lighted on
a length of old hosepipe. 'I'll let you know when it's
ready. We can shoot at your mother. Joking!' she added
hastily when she saw Janey's face.

'Or,' said Janey darkly, 'at fighter jets. Get ready,
G-Mamma. There's something going on up there. And
I'm going to find out what it is.'

It was a mission for Jane Blonde. She was going,
that night, and nothing and nobody were going to stop
her.

4 meltdown

Unfortunately for Janey, she'd forgotten about the two most influential people in her world.

She found both her parents in their Spylab, poring over something Janey couldn't see.

'What are you doing?' she said, and they both turned around with a start.

'Looking at a map,' said her father, rolling it up into a tube and smiling at Janey. 'We're thinking about another holiday, as Florida wasn't exactly restful.'

She jumped on the end of the bed. 'No! You can't go away! Something has happened.' Janey told them what she had just heard on the news.

Her parents looked at each other. 'That sounds serious,' said her mother steadily. 'I could go up to Sol's Lols tonight and check.'

Janey drew in a sharp breath. Of course, she was delighted that her mum was now keen to get involved in missions, but *she'd* unearthed this one. 'Can't I go?'

Her father held up his hand. 'Nobody's going. We can check it out from a distance. Anyway, I'm sure one of my employees would have told me if there was a major problem.' He pulled up a company organization chart on the computer screen. It showed two columns: undercover SPIs and the people who actually produced the lollies.

Janey shook her head. 'One of us needs to go, surely.' Why was he so reluctant to go and have a look?

Her father watched her face carefully for a moment, then said, 'All right, but it should be me. If there are frightened employees, or even scared SPIs, then their boss should be the one to talk to them. Jean, you can come with me.'

'But – I know Sol's Lols really well,' argued Janey. 'I've been there twice, and I'd be able to see immediately if something's changed.'

'Janey, nothing will have changed,' said her father. 'It's more than likely that this story is about exactly what it says it is.'

'A pelican? A pelican in a jet?' Janey could hear her voice getting shrill, and tried not to notice her mum folding her arms across her chest in a don't-take-that-tone-with-me-young-lady fashion. 'They don't have pelicans in Scotland, do they?' She whisked around and tapped into the computer. 'No. See. There. No pelicans, and someone in a jet doing test runs over Sols Lols.'

'Janey . . .' warned Jean.

Boz simply shrugged. 'Well, if there is anything funny about it, your mum and I will find out.'

'What shall I do?' said Janey plaintively.

'You can look after James,' said her mum.

'Look after *James*?' Janey could hardly believe her ears. 'Mum, just this morning you told me that Jamie doesn't need looking after.'

'He does when his new parents are out on dangerous missions.'

Janey felt a horrible familiar tingling across the bridge of her nose. 'So you admit that it's dangerous. Something *is* going on, and I'm not being silly,' she said quietly, not daring to raise her voice. She knew that if she got any angrier, she would surely, definitely, burst into tears.

There was a long pause in which Jean and Boz looked at each other uncomfortably.

'Listen,' said her mother eventually, 'we just don't want you to get hurt if . . . and it's only an if . . .'

'If? Get hurt?' Janey knew she was shouting now, but she couldn't help herself. 'You know you can trust my spy instincts! Look at our previous missions. I'm always right in the end – about the Sinerlesse, and about Copernicus or his henchmen every creepy time he's shown up at a different location: here, the

Hallidays', Sol's Lols, Antarctica, Dubbo Seven and Solfari Lands and . . . and . . . Sunny Jim's Swims and even on a new planet with the Lay-Z Beam. And I've nearly died so . . . so many times, and every time I've come through it. Me! Jane Blonde, Sensational Spylet! Jane Blonde should be the one going on this mission!'

And then the unthinkable happened. Her father, his shoulders hunched in fury, flailed across the lab, shoving test tubes and gadgetry off the benches in a frenzy. 'No!' he bellowed. 'I will go – on my own. I am still the head of this organization, and I decide who does what, and I am still . . . your –' he roared as he smacked his fist down on the bench – '*father!*'

At which point Janey finally burst into tears. 'I . . . I hate you!' she screamed, flinging herself down the SPIral staircase.

As she reached the bottom of the stairs James was coming up the front path. He stared at her, bewildered. Janey brushed her angry tears aside and shoved past him, whispering, 'Sorry.' Whatever had happened, it wasn't James's fault. But she'd never been so furious – and confused – in all her life, and she didn't know what to do with herself. So she slammed the gate behind her, took to the streets and ran.

Running calmed her down. Janey was not as fast as she was with her Fleet-feet on, by any means, nor was she particularly graceful. But it still felt good to be burning through the streets. By the time she'd run out of breath, she'd also run out of anger. Instead, a cool instinctive logic had taken over. As well as the weird pelican and fighter jet story, her father's uncharacteristic behaviour indicated that something was up. Whether she was allowed or not, Jane Blonde was going to have to check this out for herself.

Returning home, she knocked on the garage door and opened it. G-Mamma was chasing Trouble around, yelling, 'Leave the birdies alone!' He'd just dropped another fluttering specimen into his tyre-nest.

'G-Mamma, can I talk to you?'

The SPI:KE skidded to a halt in front of her, her cheeks more rosy than ever. She blew a curl out of her eye. 'That's what I'm here for. At least, I think it is. It used to be. Now nobody seems to . . . to . . . Even the cat's disobeying me.' And to Janey's shock a fat tear tipped over on to G-Mamma's cheek and streaked its way through her make-up. 'Sorry, Blonde. Something in my eye . . .'

Janey nodded. 'I know, G-Mamma. I understand. I . . . I got something in my eye earlier. Dad . . .' She didn't really know what to think about her father. 'I think he might be losing it a bit. He got so angry with me.'

'Yes. He's been a little touchy with me too, I have to say,' said G-Mamma with a sniff. 'Anyway, what's your point?'

Janey stared at her reflection in the mirrored wall. Janey Brown. So ordinary. But rather extraordinary beneath it all. 'I think we need to take matters into our own hands,' she said quietly.

'No,' said G-Mamma in a flat voice. 'We can't. Boz has always been the boss man.'

'But there's something going on. He's not behaving normally. He's chucked you out of your lab and now he's shouting at me. He won't let me go on the mission to Sol's Lols. So . . .' Janey peeped up at her SPI:KE, holding her breath, '. . . I think I should go anyway, with your help.'

G-Mamma regarded her thoughtfully for a moment. 'OK, Blonday,' she said slowly. 'Looks like we both need to find ourselves a new job. Let's do it! Just until we're sure your dad's OK,' she added hastily.

'Deal,' said Janey. A minute later she walked back into the house, apologized to her parents and promised to look after James as they had asked.

Bedtime seemed to take forever to come around, following a half-finished game of Monopoly that everyone soon tired of. But at long last she was in her bedroom. Putting on her pyjama shorts and top in case anyone checked on her, she inserted the SPI-Pod G-Mamma had given her into her ear, moved some books out of the way and pushed her ear up against the wall between her room and the Spylab.

She had almost nodded off, upright, when she

heard the first sounds she had been listening out for
– the dull *thunk* of the Wower door shutting, and her
father's voice, barely audible, saying 'Wow me.' Some
minutes later her mother's voice warned him to be careful – 'You know how weak it makes you. SPIV me when
you want to come back' – and then there was the tiniest
splintering noise accompanied by a low *zummmm* as the
Satispy sprang into action.

Janey leaped into bed as she heard her mother
coming through the tunnel to her bedroom. For a tiny
moment she felt Jean staring at her, and she tried hard
not to let her eyelids flicker, but at last the bedroom
door opened and closed, and Janey sat up.

She gave it ten seconds, then lunged for the
fireplace. The Wower cast its spell over her with its
wonderful robotic arms and haze of spy-making droplets, and moments later Jane Blonde stepped out and
hissed into the SPI Visualator hanging around her
neck. 'G-Mamma, I'm ready.'

'Right with you, Blondette, any second now,' came
the reply, and then suddenly . . . *DOOF!* G-Mamma
was sprawled across the windowsill, her face in the sink
and her legs waving around in the night air outside.
'Help me in,' she spluttered.

Janey dragged G-Mamma through and on to the
floor. She handed her SPI:KE the remote control for
the Satispy, after tapping in the now familiar coord-
inates of the Sol's Lols headquarters. But G-Mamma

fiddled with the control, panting, 'I've had a brainwave – let's head straight for the RAF base. Then we won't bump into your weirdy beardy father at Sol's Lols, and we can check out this pelican business for ourselves. If we find the jet planes, we can get straight to the enemy.'

Janey had to admit it made sense.

'You first. I'll see you there in three minutes.' G-Mamma pointed the remote at her and pressed the release button. Janey would be there in no time, her stream of cells shooting out through the skylight and zinging down right behind the building.

Moments later Jane Blonde plopped on to the ground. She could see the ice-lolly-shaped Sol's Lols building lit up in the distance. In the next instant there was a thump next to her. G-Mamma let out a low groan. 'Splatterspy, not Satispy – that's what they should call that. Always makes me feel so sick.'

G-Mamma pulled on her diamanté-encrusted Ultra-gogs and searched around in the darkness. 'Aircraft hangars are across there. Let's ASPIC our way over and investigate.'

Janey removed her sleek Aeronautical SPI Conveyor from her thigh. G-Mamma whipped hers out from up a voluminous trouser leg, and they pushed off together across the grass, checking the distances and outlines of the buildings through their Ultra-gogs as they passed. The miles raced beneath their ASPICs in as many seconds, and very soon they were sliding to a halt outside the hangars.

'X-ray,' said Janey to her Ultra-gogs, panning around so she could see inside each of the three enormous sheds.

'No sign of the jet from the news – these planes are all new, undamaged. Hang on, though – they wouldn't put a broken plane in with the others, would they?'

G-Mamma grinned, her teeth pale in the moonlight. 'And that is why . . . you're a Blondette spy,' she said with evident satisfaction. 'Good thinking. Let's look for a little plane graveyard.'

'Or a workshop,' said Janey. 'Um, seek!' she said. Luckily G-Mamma had preprogrammed the computer image of the battered fighter jet into the Gogs, and after a few minutes of whirring and clicking the spy glasses locked on to something and bleeped loudly.

'There,' said Janey, scooting off on her ASPIC as soon as the map pinged up on the glass of her Ultra-gogs display.

G-Mamma pushed off behind her, and together they made their way to an old, slightly rusty hangar, far out across the fields. It didn't even have any chicken wire around it to protect it, so they whizzed straight up to the tired old building. 'Looks rather like my new Spylab,' said G-Mamma stiffly.

The plane looked awful, with a savaged nose and bits of wire and metal hanging out like severed

33

veins. 'Oh, poor thing,' said G-Mamma. 'It could do with a turn in a Wower.'

Next to it was another plane, smaller and not obviously damaged, but with a huge amount of white sticky tape wound across the undercarriage. 'This one needs work too, by the looks of it,' said Janey.

G-Mamma was just moving forward to take a look when something erupted behind her with a muffled *crump*. Janey staggered into the SPI:KE as the ground beneath their feet juddered. Nearby, the damaged fighter plane creaked, groaned and collapsed on its side.

'What in the name of pet jets was that?' squeaked G-Mamma.

Janey had already run outside and zoomed in with her Ultra-gogs, her throat closing up with terror. It was every bit as bad as she'd feared. 'Look, G-Mamma. It's Sol's Lols!'

G-Mamma raced to her side. 'What's up with the lolly?'

They focused together on the distant structure. It was still there. Just. But it appeared to have melted. The whole 'stick' of the lolly, in which the reception area had been housed, had completely disappeared, and now the rest of the building was resting a little drunkenly on the ground. Flames licked through the lower windows, as though the building itself was breathing fire.

meltdown

'They might not have succeeded earlier,' said Janey sombrely, 'but they've definitely blown it up now.'

'But – the Boz man might be in there!'

Janey jumped on to her hoverboard. 'Let's go.'

'Not on these plastic ASPICs. It'll take too long. We only have seconds. Come on!' G-Mamma pelted for the little fighter jet – the one that was still standing.

'No! G-Mamma, you can't . . .'

But of course she could. And Janey ran after the SPI:KE, not knowing which was more scary – that they were about to take off in a plane that was held together by white tape like a hospital patient . . .

. . . or that the pilot was G-Mamma.

# 5 up and out

Janey had little choice but to strap herself in behind G-Mamma, who jabbed at buttons until the perspex lid above them lowered itself into position and clunked shut. Then she pressed something else, seemingly at random, and crowed with delight as the engine burst into life.

Janey tapped her on the shoulder. 'Where's the runway?'

G-Mamma peered round at her blankly and then turned away. Of course. She couldn't hear anything above the roar of the jet. Reaching into one of her hidden pockets, Janey extracted the SPI-Pod, tucked an earphone into G-Mamma's ear and turned it up to maximum volume. 'I said, where's the runway?'

She popped the other earphone into her own ear just in time to hear G-Mamma saying '. . . This baby . . . directs the turbine outflow through positional nozzles in the fuselage and wings. Takes off vertically like a helicopter. It's up and out, Blonderini. Yeehah!'

Amazingly, it did appear that G-Mamma knew what she was doing. They taxied out to the space in front of the hangar, circled a few times while the SPI:KE got the hang of the controls and then she screamed, 'G-force from the G-Mamma!' and thrust down on the gear stick. Janey squeaked, expecting them to shoot into the air, but instead they lifted gently off the ground, the wings tipping slightly this way and that as they rose above the airfield. G-Mamma took her hand off the throttle long enough to give Janey an exhilarated thumbs-up, then she pressed in a button on the handle, and BOOM! They were off.

'G-Maaaaaaaa . . .'

Janey tried to focus as her face was sucked into the back of her head. In the blur that streaked below them she could see various RAF personnel skidding out of the buildings, looking up at them, then running for the hangars, but milliseconds later they were gone. Green paddocks, cows, lakes, buildings, all melded into a multi-coloured stripe as the earth fell away beneath them.

'I'm taking it to the max!' screamed G-Mamma, corkscrewing through the low clouds. 'Nearly seven hundred miles an hour . . . TO THE MAX!'

And as her head bent backwards over the seat and her voice became rather strangulated, Janey managed to yell, 'G-Mamma, we've overshot!'

'What?'

Janey pointed backwards and G-Mamma adjusted her Ultra-gogs. 'Oops. Forgot. Sorry.'

The smouldering Sol's Lols building was a mere glimmer about fifty miles behind them. 'Quickest way back!' she hollered, then looped the loop twice and set off in the opposite direction, upside down. Janey laughed aloud as G-Mamma whooped and yelled, 'It's a blast, Blonde-girl!'

'We're nearly there! Slow down.'

The engines groaned as G-Mamma geared down for landing. She aimed for the Sol's Lols car park, jabbing at a button, and then turned pale. 'Um, Blonde,' she said indistinctly as she rattled the keys, buttons and levers before her, 'I might have discovered why the jet was in the workshop.'

There was an odd tugging sensation beneath Janey's seat, and the terrible grating sounds of a snared-up mechanism. 'The wheels don't come down, do they?' said Janey as they lurched and pitched above the car park.

'They're just a teensy bit stuck,' confessed G-Mamma.

'So if we land we're just a teensy bit dead?'

'Sort of. We could eject. But then the plane would be out of control. And we're a bit low on fuel.'

'Low?'

'Well . . . empty.'

'Great. And now we've got company.' Janey looked up as a V-shaped formation of fighter jets shot overhead. 'Open the roof thingy,' she said firmly, 'hold her steady and give me your ASPIC.'

The wind nearly ripped her head off as the perspex slid back. They were still bobbing around like a puppet on a string somewhere above the car park. Still in formation, the jets were turning around in the distance, heading back towards them. Tucking G-Mamma's ASPIC under her arm, Janey unclipped her seat belt and hoisted herself over the rim of the cockpit. Now there was just air, turbulent and dense with diesel fumes, between her and the ground a hundred feet below. 'Aaagh!' She grabbed on firmly with her Girl-gauntlet as the plane lunged to one side.

'Sorreee,' she heard faintly from above.

The stench from the engines was revolting. Janey grabbed the end of her silky ponytail and wrapped it across her face to cut out the fumes, then slowly . . . slowly . . . she lowered herself down by extending her arm. Now she was hanging from the cockpit down the side of the plane, arm fully stretched. 'Don't fail me now, Fleet-feet,' she whispered. Then, forcing one leg against the tumultuous wind that threatened to rip her away from the plane at any second, she moved her foot towards the fuselage.

Clunk.

It held fast, magnetized to the metal carcass

of the jet. Swallowing hard, Janey counted to three and then swung herself out through the drag, fixing her other foot next to the first in the same movement. This had to be about the maddest thing she'd ever done – now she was hanging upside down, by the feet, from the bottom of a hovering fighter jet. Only her spygear was preventing her from being plucked off like a petal from a flower and whisked away through the clouds to an ugly death.

But it was working. 'OK, move,' Janey told herself and, step by agonizing step, she forced herself towards the tape-covered hatch from which the wheels should have descended.

A tinny voice rang out from somewhere above her: 'Blonde, hurry up!'

'Head for the Sol's Lols moat,' she screamed, hoping desperately that G-Mamma would hear her as she doubled herself upwards and, with the titanium blade in her Girl-gauntlet, prised away the taped hatch, utilizing every scrap of the spy-glove's amazing strength. She stared, horrifed. It was as she'd secretly feared – the wheels weren't just jammed. They were missing.

Luckily Jane Blonde had foreseen this eventuality.

'OK, ASPICs, do your job,' she said. Then she eased the plane's metal legs out of their housing, straining with the effort until her eyes felt as though they were about to burst from her skull. It seemed like hours but was really only seconds later that she felt a satisfying click. The legs had snapped into position.

'They're coming!' screeched G-Mamma in the SPIV.

Janey grasped her ASPIC and anchored it to the bottom of one of the wheel gantreys. It held fast, magnetized by its powerful SPI technology.

'There's one right over us! It's going to . . . Hang on!'

Trying to keep calm, to hang on as the plane bobbed across to the moat, Janey fixed G-Mamma's ASPIC into place.

'That one's not a plane. It's that pelican thing!' screeched G-Mamma.

Janey scrambled up the side of the plane as fast as the lurching, wobbling aircraft and her magnetic Fleet-feet would allow. 'Never mind, G-Mamma. You've got skis like a seaplane. Land on the moat. Now!'

She glanced upwards as the plane swooped alarmingly. G-Mamma was right. There was a large bird's wing – not just large, enormous – sliding out of view into the clouds. But hadn't the news said that the pelican was presumed dead?

Suddenly Janey's insides flew up into her throat as if she was on a roller-coaster.

'We're . . . down!' screamed G-Mamma. Then, with a final lurch and a spray of water, G-Mamma sat the jet on the moat, killed the engine and unbuckled herself, all in the same frantic movement. 'JUMP!'

As Jane Blonde leaped off one side and her SPI:KE threw herself off the other, their little jet, too heavy for the ASPICs to support, started to sink. Then they heard a screech of tyres. Shouting. Car doors opening.

Fumbling in the water, Janey chewed her SPIder – the rubbery creepy-crawly device that would squirt oxygen into her lungs – and dived below the surface. Instantly her Ultra-gogs responded to the environment, sealing around her eyes so that she could see clearly. There, floating nearby like an enormous Ultra-gogged jellyfish, was G-Mamma, furiously chewing her own SPIder. Janey gave her the universal diving buddy sign, and G-Mamma followed her round to the pipe that Janey knew led to the swimming pool in the Sol's Lols building . . .

But she'd never seen it like this.

There was no swimming pool. As they were half-way along the tunnel, which now lay at a steep angle, blown off course by the explosion, the water ran out.

'They've blown up the Spylab,' Janey whispered, hardly able to take it in. While the main building still looked more or less intact, the basement Spylab had been completely obliterated. Reception had disappeared into a deep bowl in the earth about the size of the school playing field. Among the debris, they could see the remains of computers and the benches they had been sitting on, a variety of SPI-buys (including a Back-boat, a set of broken ASPICs and some bricks of blackened SPInamite) and the top of what looked like a Wower cubicle.

Footsteps rang out above them.

'Someone's coming. That could be Dad,' Janey said quickly.

G-Mamma looked at her for a moment, then nodded. 'Right. We need to get to that reception desk.'

'I'll go,' said Janey.

She would have preferred to have her ASPIC to get across the gaping maw that used to be the Spylab, but that was now anchored at the bottom of the moat beneath several tons of fighter jet; instead she operated her Fleet-feet jump, flew as far as she could across the abyss, then swung across using the wires and bits of metal that hung from the caved-in ceiling.

She quickly located and switched on the security footage leading up to the explosion. 'I'll project this through my SPIV so you can see it, G-Mamma,' she whispered. 'Scan and save,' she told her Ultra-gogs.

The footage showed the guard on reception shouting on the phone. 'Four-minute warning!' he was yelling, frantically pulling things out of the desk. 'We've got to get out. Get everyone out!' He grabbed the intercom and shouted, 'Emergency! All employees to clear the building immediately. Immediately!' and then he hurdled the desk and headed for the door.

The next minute or so was confusing, with people in white coats – the SPI team – spilling out of offices and through the door and huddling together beyond the moat. And then the explosion, a vast *WHUMP*, like the biggest firework ever experienced, a blinding light and thunderous crashing sound, and then the building settling slowly like a long skirt around the smoking, smouldering remains of the Spylab.

That was all. Blackness. Apart from . . . 'Blonde, play that bit again,' said G-Mamma quickly. It looked like a tail, but not of any animal Janey knew. It was long, high and . . . scaly? The security camera followed it as far as the woodland surrounding the building, but then the screen went blank. Just as the image faded, Janey thought she saw another figure in the trees, or rather a pair of legs. Short legs. Legs she'd seen somewhere before.

Before she had a chance to rewind and watch it again, a voice shouted, 'Who's there?'

Her father. Relief and panic flooded through her.

Janey heard G-Mamma gulp, then rattle off instructions into her SPIV. 'Blonde, I'll send you home with the remote. Go straight to bed, and don't let anyone know you've been out. We'll decode tomorrow.'

As Janey disintegrated she wondered how they'd decode, when she really had no idea what it was she'd just seen.

6 too many spies

No sooner had she flung herself into bed, still in her SPIsuit, than there was the sound of a struggle on the SPIral staircase next door. Janey whisked through the fireplace tunnel, dropped down into a combat position and prepared for battle.

Then she heard who it was. 'But I've *always* been the Satipsy operator, while you were mopping floors!' G-Mamma's voice was shrill with indignation.

'I was only mopping floors because I didn't know who I was!' Thud . . . bang . . . The two SPIs fought to beat each other to the top of the narrow staircase. 'And who I am is . . . get off! . . . Gina Bellarina . . . OW! . . . and wife of Boz!'

Janey stared as two flushed faces popped up at the top of the stairs. 'Mum, G-Mamma . . . what are you doing?'

In the same instant and with the same motion, both women smoothed down their hair and stalked with fake politeness into the Spylab.

'After you, Jean . . .'

'No, no, you first, Rosie.'

Suddenly Janey knew exactly what she must look like when she got caught doing something she shouldn't. 'You'll wake Jamie up,' she said, trying to buy G-Mamma some time. She'd obviously arrived back at the very same moment that her mum had been about to operate the Satispy to retrieve Boz.

'Oh, of course.' Jean had the grace to look very shamefaced, but then her eyes narrowed. 'But what . . . what are you doing here, Janey?'

'Oh, well, I heard all the kerfuffle from next door and thought I'd better come and see what was going on.' More lies, she thought guiltily.

Her mother checked her over suspiciously. 'You're in your SPIsuit.'

'I just had time to Wow. I thought you might be an enemy!'

Just then a deep voice called out from the SPIV around Jean's neck, 'Will *somebody* Satispy me home, please?'

At that there was an ungainly grapple for the remote control; Jean reached it first, pressing the red button triumphantly. By the time Boz materialized in front of them, he was faced with two red-faced angry spies, each trying to stare the other down.

'I've *always* been your Satispy operator,' repeated

G-Mamma, even before Boz's hair had time to re-attach itself. 'Always.'

Janey's father recovered himself as quickly as possible. 'Ah, well, Jean was right here, so it just seemed simpler to ask—'

'But *I* would have been right here if you hadn't packed me of to Garage Gaga-land.'

'That's true. Not that I packed you off to . . . but you are always right here for me, G-Mamma, and that means a huge amount to me.'

'And to me!' piped up Janey, concerned for her SPI:KE. G-Mamma had folded her arms across her great bosom and was quivering with fury.

Gina Bellarina put her hand on G-Mamma's arm. 'I'm sorry,' she said. 'This is all so exciting to me, I get a bit carried away.'

Although Janey's mum sounded completely sincere, G-Mamma shook off her hand as if it was a leech. 'I wish you would be,' she said, her chin wobbling madly as she fought back tears. 'Carried away, I mean. Completely away. Nothing's been the same since you remembered your spy life. Nothing!' Trying to stop herself crying again, she spun around towards the SPIral staircase. 'If you do ever think of anything you need me for, I'll be in my GARAGE. Or . . . better yet, down under at Dubbo Seven. At least there the sheep like me.' And with a great gargling sniff, she disappeared.

Janey glared at her parents. 'Aren't you going after her?' she said quietly.

Her mother shook her head. 'Even if I did, I wouldn't be able to say the right thing.'

'Dad?'

'I will. I can see I've not handled things very well. But before that . . .' He patted Janey on the shoulder. 'You were right. The Sol's Lols headquarters has been damaged.'

'Damaged?' echoed Janey, incredulous. 'Completely blown apart, don't you mean?' Then she remembered that she wasn't supposed to have seen it. 'Er . . . at least, that's what I thought they were hinting at on that news programme,' she added hastily.

'No, it's repairable,' said her father. 'Most of it is glass and stuff that can be replaced. And nobody was hurt, which is the most important thing.'

Janey was nothing short of baffled. His entire main Spylab had disappeared into a great big hole. Yet her father seemed to be implying that there were just a few broken windows.

'Good job, Blonde, alerting us to this. Gina and I are going to go and check out the other Spylabs, starting with Solfari Lands, just to make sure they're OK. In the meantime, keep an eye on the news and on James, will you?'

Jean nodded at Janey to press the button on the remote control; after a slight pause she pushed it and waved to her disintegrating parents.

★

There was no point protesting. For some reason she and G-Mamma were being excluded from the plans for SPI. Janey could hardly believe it, but her spying gut reactions had taken over now and she felt calm and capable. She and G-Mamma would work as a team and sort this thing out.

Though there was one new team member who still needed initiating . . .

As soon as the last particle of her father had disappeared she padded across the Spylab, silent in her Fleet-feet, and headed downstairs to James's room. 'It's me,' she hissed into the darkness.

James sat up, the duvet dropping from his shoulders. Janey laughed. He was wearing his pyjama top, but there was a deep V of gleaming black and white visible on his chest. 'You love being a spy so much you're sleeping in your SPIsuit?'

James grinned and shrugged.

'Me too,' said Janey, pointing down at her silvery legs.

For about an hour they chatted in a rather one-sided conversation, since James could only answer Janey in signs and mimes. They agreed, however, that their father was behaving strangely, and that he should be letting them investigate more. Agent Sable was desperate to go on his first mission. There was nothing more they could do tonight though, and to her surprise Janey snuggled down at the end of James's bed and fell sound asleep.

It was breakfast time before the two of them met up with their parents again. Both Boz and Jean were acting very nonchalant.

'How was Solfari Lands?' said Janey, helping herself to cereal.

'Fine,' said her father brightly, although his voice sounded a little thick, as if he had a cold coming on.

'So . . . what about the other Spylabs?' continued Janey as her mother smiled at James and spread peanut butter on his toast. 'And have you discovered who was behind the bombing of Sol's Lols?'

'Let's worry about all that later, shall we?' said Jean. 'Concentrate on breakfast.'

'But how many other Spylabs—'

'Not now, Janey,' said her father firmly.

It was all she could do not to glare at him. Thank goodness for G-Mamma, she thought, biting her RaisinBix savagely. She couldn't wait to debrief. And she was taking James with her. They couldn't make him into a Spylet and then refuse to let him do anything. 'Let's play football,' she said to James, but she winked broadly at him, and moments later they were heading off across the garden.

G-Mamma was stepping out of the Wower when they arrived. 'Just de-Wowed,' she told them. 'I had a busy night after I got back.'

Janey was just relieved to see her there. 'I was worried you might actually have gone to Dubbo Seven.'

'No, that was a small bending of the truth, my little Spiblings – that's SPI siblings to you. I took the spy-tube from the underground at the bottom of the road – did you know Bozzy-babe has set it up on the planetary circuit? – and the first stop was Florida.'

'To visit NASA,' said Janey with a nod.

'Correct. But . . .' G-Mamma leaned in, her round face burning with a massive secret so that Janey thought she rather resembled a Jammy Dodger, 'it wasn't there!'

James gulped audibly, and Janey could quite understand why. 'What wasn't there? Cape Canaveral?'

'Well, obviously, Jane the brain, it might have been on the news if the whole of the space centre had disappeared. No,' said G-Mamma, 'the Spylab. The one Copernicus was using. It's gone.'

'Disappeared?'

G-Mamma leaned in still further. 'I think it was blown up too. There was this big pile of rubble, with loads of scaffolding around the outside holding up the rest of the building.'

'Just like at Sol's Lols,' said Janey.

When she glanced at her new little brother Janey noticed that he looked close to tears. She raised her eyebrows at him, and in response he curved his hand into a large letter. 'C. Big C. Oh.' Janey suddenly understood the cause of his concern.

'Jamie's worried that Copernicus has escaped from Cape Canaveral.' When they'd last seen him, their squid-shaped arch-enemy had been in stasis, suspended in a shower-like tank that kept him barely alive.

'Don't be afraid, Able Sable. Oooo.' G-Mamma's eyes gleamed. 'Don't be afraid, Able Sable. Don't hide yourself beneath the table. It's gonna be fine, oh Spylet mine . . . Oh, all right, I'll stop,' she said, catching Janey's warning look. 'It really is fine though. Old One-eyed Squinty Squid is still in his tank, right where we left him.'

So if Copernicus was still safely out of the way, who was going round blowing up Spylabs? And where would they strike next? 'Mum and Dad told me they had been to Solfari Lands, but I don't trust anything they say these days.'

'They did go. Oop! I mean, I expect they did.' G-Mamma looked a bit shifty.

'How do you know where Mum and Dad were?'

'Just guessed,' said G-Mamma, staring at the ceiling.

'G-Mamma . . .'

'Oh, OK, keep your gauntlet on.' G-Mamma looked around, spotted Trouble curled up on the bed in the corner and whistled to him. 'I'm a spy, aren't I? Have to keep up with what's going on.'

Trouble jumped up on to the bench top and G-Mamma pointed to the Spycat's collar. It had changed. Instead of being decorated with metal studs, there were now four silvery eyes, complete with false eyelashes, spread out along its length. As Janey looked, one of them blinked, rotated and fixed itself on the body appearing behind them in the Spylab. Instantly the image projected itself on to G-Mamma's huge SPIV screen.

Janey could hardly believe what she was seeing as another of the eyes swivelled towards her, and her stunned face appeared briefly on the SPIV before her. 'What is that?'

'I'm calling it a Cat's Eye Collar.' G-Mamma shoved Trouble off the bench and out of sight as Boz's ears came into view on the screen. 'My latest invention! And I know it works because Trouble went on a little mission of his own, and spied your parents going into Solfari Lands.'

'Er . . . Clever.' Janey shuddered in disgust as Trouble preened in his newest accessory, rubbing against her leg. 'Yes, Twubs, you look . . . er . . . gorgeous. We've come to debrief.'

'Decode, debrief, de-Wow, oh yeah,' rapped G-Mamma nodding. 'But quite honestly, I don't know what else we can say at the moment. Someone's blowing up Spylabs. We just have to get to them first.'

'The RAF?'

G-Mamma shook her head. 'Why would the Royal Air Force be involved?'

'They chased us though.'

'I think they were just upset we stole their jet. Oh!' G-Mamma's eyes sparkled as she scrolled through news items on the computer. 'Look.'

And she rapped gently as Janey read the news report on the mysterious theft and loss of a damaged fighter jet:

'We stole their jet,
They were very upset,
Now we've dropped it in the moat
And that REALLY got their goat . . .'

The news item looked very serious. The RAF were talking about possible terrorist attacks – and whether this was linked to the explosions at Sol's Lols and at NASA.

'Oh dear,' said Janey. 'We'd better be a bit more careful from now on. It's not like we can get SPI to cover for us, as Dad didn't know we were there.'

G-Mamma checked the surveillance camera on the fridge door. 'Speak of the devil! Daddy's here. Crikey, what's wrong with him?'

'He must have hurt his back,' said Janey, peering over G-Mamma's shoulder. 'He's been looking a bit hunched over like that for a few days.'

'Well, any more and he'll be able to ring the bells at Notre Dame,' said G-Mamma with a sneer. 'Greetings, dear leader!' she said with false brightness as Boz opened the door.

He smiled at her and nodded hello. 'Come on, kids,' he said, pointing back at the house. 'Time to de-Wow. Your mum wants to take you out shopping.'

Janey rolled her eyes at G-Mamma. Shopping?! When one by one the Spylabs were being taken out by a mysterious new enemy? She sighed. It was almost as if her spy life was disappearing. As if, in fact, her parents wanted it to.

sparrow storm

It wasn't all bad though, because, much to his disgust, Alfie needed uniform too. In a low voice Janey filled him in on recent events. He was incensed that he hadn't got to fly in a fighter jet, but completely bewildered when Janey described how cross her mum and dad had been.

'Is that all?' Alfie shook his head in wonderment. 'You're *wayyy* too sensitive. Mum says stuff like that to me all the time.'

'But mine doesn't,' said Janey, trying to ignore her dull reflection in a shop window as they passed. She sighed. 'Maybe you're right. I'm just not used to it.'

Alfie tapped the side of his nose. 'Trust your Uncle Alfie. I know lots about crabby parents. Just forget about it.'

There was more to it than that, she felt, but she would keep her concerns to herself. 'So what do boys have to wear at Everdene?' she said, changing the subject to their new secondary school.

Alfie fumbled in his pocket for the uniform list. 'Erm, trousers and pullover in a shade of snotty green, shirt and tie in puke green. Tie in both colours – stripes of snot and stripes of puke.'

Janey giggled. 'I think that's bottle green and pale lime. We've got dark green skirts for the winter, and dresses for the summer in lime.'

'You'll look disgusting,' said Alfie pleasantly, pushing through the door of Seacrest and Argents. 'Well, here we are. They'll have your uniform here too, Jamie. Nice normal navy blue. See how kind my mum is.'

As headmistress of Winton Primary, Mrs Halliday had done a good job of choosing a neutral uniform. Janey could pass down her jumpers to her little brother, but he was going to need trousers and shorts in place of her skirts and pinafores. James looked around, expectantly.

'I'll let you into a secret,' said Janey, whispering directly into her little brother's ear. 'At night this becomes a store for secret agents; we can get all our SPI-buys in here.'

James's eyes grew round, and he watched carefully as someone went into a changing cubicle. When they came out looking exactly the same his disappointment was obvious. 'Only at night,' repeated Janey.

By night, when the extra letters dropped away from the Seacrest and Argents shop sign to become 'Secret Agents', the store became a cornucopia of wonderful gadgets and spy outfits, from the tiniest spy rings and rocket hairslides to an eight-seater Back-boat. Right at that moment, however, it looked like an ordinary high-street department store, with 'Back to School!' posters plastered all over the walls.

The whole shopping experience was very ordinary too, the only highlight being when Alfie stepped miserably out of a changing room wearing a jumper with enormous dangly sleeves.

'That's the one,' said Mrs Halliday.

'*Mu-um!* I look like an ape – oh, sorry, James. No offence. But look, the sleeves droop down to my knees!'

But his mother was already hauling it over his head and dropping it into her shopping basket. 'Room to grow, Alfie. I'm not buying you a new jumper every few months.'

'But, Mum, I . . .'

At which point Mrs Halliday snapped, 'That's enough!' and Alfie shot Janey an 'I told you so' expression.

Trying not to laugh at her friend's misery, Janey wandered over to the back wall to look at the shoes. They were endlessly sensible – brown and black with boring buckles and laces. G-Mamma would hate them, thought Janey. She sighed, staring out the window.

Suddenly, to her amazement, there *was* G-Mamma, in a side street outside, looking left and right, right and left, then taking to her heels and running like a maniac towards the high street and out of view.

Immediately Janey climbed up on the middle shelf of shoes so that she could see further. G-Mamma's quivering back was disappearing into the distance, chasing something – a large bird? An enormous turkey! The biggest one from the allotment! Trouble was in hot pursuit, streaking along the pavement, swerving between shoppers' feet like a heat-seeking missile. As Janey stared, stunned, she distinctly saw one of the cat's eyes on his collar swivel in her direction for a moment, and then spin away to look at something else.

But wait – Trouble was being chased too! Something was buzzing after him . . . Was that a swarm of bees? With a whistling sound that Janey could hear even through the window, one of the small objects shot past her and after the cat, followed by another, then another, like a fistful of darts. Birds!

As Janey watched, open-mouthed, worried that Trouble was in trouble, one of the birds flew round in a circle, coming up at the rear of the flock, then angled itself in a different direction. Not after Trouble. After Janey. Before she could react, the bird had opened its mouth; not cheeping but croaking, rasping, it flung itself straight at her face . . .

It hit the window with a *smack-crack*, then

tumbled to the ground, but not before Janey had managed to see that the bird had been aiming to tear her face off. It looked like a sparrow. It flew like a sparrow. But this thing had teeth! Needle-sharp racks of teeth, like a tiny flying shark.

Then she remembered a cricket stump with feathers on the end. Was *this* the SParrow that her SPI:KE had been working on? 'Oh, G-Mamma,' she groaned. 'What are you up to now?'

'What is she up to?' said a voice behind her.

Janey jumped, almost tumbling from the shelf of shoes. 'Mum! You frightened me.'

'You frightened me, disappearing out of Winter Woollens and climbing halfway up a wall. Get down, please.' Janey's mother gave her a look. 'What's going on?'

Janey took a deep breath. How she'd longed to be able to do this – tell her mum everything, share all her spying adventures, live their spy life together . . . and yet she held back. She didn't want to say anything that might possibly get G-Mamma into trouble. Instead she held up a particularly revolting brown sandal. 'Just . . . I was wondering what G-Mamma's up to at the moment, because she might have time to do something with these hideous shoes. Maybe put them through the Wower.'

'Good idea – they are horrible, aren't they?' Jean laughed.

Janey nodded. She didn't like lying to her mother, but somehow her spy instincts told her it was the right thing to do. For now.

They joined the others in Boy's Clothes, paid for their purchases and made their way down the high street. Two shoppers were complaining about bird poo on their coats, and one man was wiping what looked like a Cadbury's Creme Egg off his bald head. 'Big flock of them – with teeth! I swear it,' he was saying loudly. 'Like vampire birds or something. Going for my neck, it was.'

Janey found her mum frowning at her with sudden suspicion. She looked around quickly for a distraction, and there it was, right beside her. 'Oh, Jamie,' she said, pulling her brother round to the display stand, 'do you want to go and visit your sister –' she dropped her voice in case a passer-by heard her – 'at the zoo?'

His little face lit up so quickly that Janey didn't know whether to feel mean for using him that way or a little envious that he never looked quite that pleased to see her.

Alfie looked glad of an activity too. 'I could go with them. Check out the Solfari Lands Spylab while we're there.'

'No need,' said Janey's mum brightly. 'Boz and I went yesterday – it's intact. But I'll happily drop you off at the zoo.'

Mrs Halliday shrugged. 'It's all right by me. I've got next year's rotas to do.'

'Call me when you're ready to come home,' said Janey's mum half an hour later as they clambered out of the back of the Clean Jean van, over all its mops and buckets. 'I'll come and get you.'

'Great,' muttered Alfie, shaking a duster off his foot. He changed his tone quickly when he realized both women were glaring at him. 'I mean, thanks. That would be really . . . great. Wish we had our SPIcicles with us,' he added in an undertone to Janey as the trio waved.

'Never mind that.' Janey tugged his sleeve urgently. 'I've got so much to tell you. The birds that man was moaning about – I saw them too!'

'The vampire birds? Ri-i-i-ight,' said Alfie, not believing a word of it.

'G-Mamma was after this turkey, with Trouble behind her, and these sparrows were chasing G-Mamma and Trouble up the street at the side of the shop. Then one turned back and tried to get me.'

'No way!'

'It's true. But I think G-Mamma invented them by mistake, so . . .' Janey stopped and looked around. 'Where's Jamie?'

'James!' shouted Alfie. He was nowhere to be seen. 'Well, you know exactly where he'll be.'

Janey nodded. 'The Primate Palace.'

But an hour later, after checking every ape, lemur and orang-utan in the whole of Solfari Lands, including James's chimp sister, Belle, they were no closer to finding him.

Janey had lost her little brother.

And suddenly the ground shook. Another bomb. Janey felt sick with terror for her little brother. 'Poor Jamie,' she said to Alfie, who was still recovering his balance. 'Please don't let him be dead.'

raptor capture

Alfie's phone rang.

'Ignore it!' shouted Janey.

But Alfie had already answered. With a grimace, he handed it to Janey. 'It's for you. Sorry,' he mouthed.

'Where are you?' Her father sounded stern, organized. Almost military. When she told him, he said, 'Have you been in the Spylab?'

'Not yet. But James has gone missing, and I think there was just another explosion.'

'I'll come and check,' barked her father. 'Stay right where you are, Janey.'

Janey almost dropped the phone, so surprised was she at his tone. Not that she had any reason to be shocked, she thought. His gruffness was becoming quite a habit.

'All right,' she said quietly, and ended the call.

Alfie put his hand on her shoulder. 'I heard that last bit. He must be a bit stressed out. Not quite himself.'

'Exactly what I was thinking,' said Janey. 'But I'm afraid there's no way Jane Blonde is staying put. Come on!'

And she sprinted off towards the Solfari Lands Spylab, housed below the Amphibian House, wishing fervently that she had her Fleet-feet on as well as the rest of her Blonde outfit.

'You'll be in big trouble,' panted Alfie as he matched her step for step, but before he could stop her he was caught off guard by his phone ringing. 'Hello?' Again he handed it over to Janey. 'It's for you.'

'Blonde!' screeched G-Mamma. 'That Cat's Eye Collar is brilliant. Brilliant! Up you popped in my SPIV, spying on me while I was chasing that stupid escaped turkey all over town.'

Janey puffed a little as they rounded the otter enclosure, still running as fast as their non-spy clothes would allow. 'I wasn't spying. Anyway, G-Mamma, now's not the time!' Janey skidded around a corner, slightly ahead of Alfie now. 'Jamie's missing, and I think the Solfari Lands Spylab has just been blown up.'

'Wait for me!'

'I can't,' said Janey. 'No time – Jamie might be in danger.'

'OK. Well, I'll be there as soon as I can,' said G-Mamma.

As fast as they could, the two Spylets pelted around the footpaths and across the flower beds, hopping on to the back of the little train that scuttled around the zoo, only to be pushed off by the alarmed parents of some toddlers in the last carriage.

'Ow!' Janey felt her ankle twinge as she hit the ground, but she didn't slow. There'd be time to sort that out later.

'Janey, look!' Alfie pointed over the perimeter hedge; it looked as though a bucket and mop were sliding along the top of it.

'Mum,' said Janey. 'Darn.' The Clean Jean van was just minutes from the car park.

'We're . . . nearly . . .' Alfie didn't even bother finishing the sentence, just lifted a shaky hand towards the entrance to the Amphibian House.

'Wait here,' gasped Janey. 'Fend them off at the door.'

'Yeah, right.' Alfie had no intention of letting Janey have all the fun, and Janey knew there was no time to argue it out. Together they ran for the entry tubes, covering for each other as first Janey, then Alfie, hurtled down the perspex tube into the Spylab on a cushion of air.

Or at least into what used to be the Spylab. 'Not here too . . .' whispered Janey, willing her eyes to adjust more quickly to the subterranean gloom.

The first Spylab she had ever seen – the place she had discovered her father for the very first time – had been reduced to a mess of smouldering embers. Dust rose in little eddies from the piles of bricks, over the toppled and fragmented benches, shattered plasma screens and glass-fronted cupboards; here and there, flames licked around the debris.

Janey panicked. 'Jamie!' she cried. 'James, are you in here?'

She clambered over a mound of rubble, pushing things to one side, digging where she could with her bare hands, and Alfie, seeing what she was doing, took another area of the former Spylab and did the same thing. For long minutes they searched, until Janey heard a sound in the far corner of the room. 'Jamie! Are you . . . ?'

Both Spylets turned to where the scrabbling noise had originated, and Janey's mouth went dry. It wasn't James who had caused the noise at all.

Alfie pointed, eyes wide, stuttering hoarsely: 'Jazz spark . . . jazz spark . . .'

'Jazz spark?' whispered Janey, shaking his arm to get him to calm down. The creature in the corner took a couple of dainty steps towards them, rolling its head, and they backed up rapidly. 'What's jazz spark?'

'No,' hissed Alfie, white-faced. '*Jurassic* . . . *Park*, you idiot! Slashy claws . . . eats your organs . . .'

And then she remembered. They'd watched the film together, and now one of its star characters was hopping around on a pile of bricks right in front of them.

A velociraptor.

'It can't be,' said Janey, looking around for a way past the creature.

'No?' Alfie picked up a rock and threw it at the raptor. The monstrous head snapped at it and then turned angrily back towards the two Spylets. 'Makes sense to me. Vampire birds this morning, velociraptors this afternoon . . .'

'And now you've made it mad,' said Janey as the raptor attempted to fly at them. 'Argh!' Just before the vicious teeth came too close, the creature lost its footing among the piles of stone and fell on its side. Moments later it was up again, stalking them, backing them into a corner.

'Maybe it's a vampire too,' whispered Alfie. 'It's eyeing up my neck.'

Janey's mind raced as she picked up a piece of metal to protect herself. They were pretty much in the corner of the room now, with no SPIsuits or gadgets to help them. They were doomed. Unless . . .

'I know,' said Janey. 'Dig!'

She threw a rock over the raptor's head to distract it, then dropped to the floor and scrabbled in the rubble. As the creature turned back in surprise, her hand seized a football-sized boulder beneath the surface. Janey yanked it as hard as she could, and to her great relief the other rubble shifted dramatically, slithering around to fill the hole that the boulder had left behind.

With the surface of the rubble moving like a lava flow, the raptor was once more thrown off balance; it fell to the ground, cawing like some crazed and enormous crow.

'Fantastic!' hissed Alfie, and Janey looked around, pleased. It wasn't often that Alfie could bring himself to compliment her. Then she realized that his eyes were wide with terror, and that he was just being his usual sarcastic self. 'Really fantastic,' he went on. 'Now there's nowhere for us to go, and it's going to be on us in seconds.'

The shifting of the floor had created great gaps all around them. They were stuck on a disintegrating island of metal and brick in the corner of the Spylab, with the velociraptor pecking at them from across the small ravine, ready to lunge at any moment. And just as the raptor took a couple of little paces left and right, like a cat rounding up a rat, Janey gasped.

'We've found it! Look at what we're standing on!' she said. 'Cover me, Alfie.'

Barely taking in his horrified expression, Janey leaped off their precipice into the surrounding rubble and turned her back on the raptor. 'What . . .' grunted Alfie as he hurled a fridge handle at the raptor . . . 'the heck . . .' as he lobbed a cremated pineapple across the crevasse . . . 'are you doing?'

'Hang on!' There was a cackle as the raptor caught the pineapple and cracked it between its jaws, then Janey found what she was digging for. The door would open only a fraction, pushed up against the debris, but she could just manage to shove her head and right arm through the gap. Then 'Wow me!' she hollered.

She had no idea whether the Wower would work with only some of her body inside and the door still open. 'Please Wow me!' she begged.

The Wower must have been damaged in the explosion, but somehow, with a slight shudder that had Alfie yelling and stamping from somewhere over her head, it managed to poke forth one robotic hand which frisked around her head for a moment, while a small mist of spy-transforming droplets rained down on her arm. Janey emerged a moment later, red-faced, with half her mousy hair now jutting out in a jagged platinum ponytail that could cause as much damage as velociraptor teeth, and the rest still dangling limply by her face. Her right hand was successfully encased in her much-loved Girl-gauntlet.

Limited as it was, the transformation didn't come a moment too soon. Just as Alfie reached down and pulled her, Gauntlet first, to stand on top of the Wower, the velociraptor let out a screech of frustration and launched itself at her legs.

'The door's still open – Wow up!' cried Janey. Alfie dangled upside down from the top of the Wower and shoved his head and one arm through the open door as

Janey crouched and turned in the same motion, her back to the monster as it lunged. Her dagger ponytail plunged into the soft flesh of the raptor's throat; there was a horrific gurgling sound and the creature fell back.

But before she even had time to be sickened by the dinosaur blood dripping off her hair, the wounded raptor was climbing the rubbly slope again, turning, lunging, snapping with its hideous teeth . . .

It flung itself across the narrow ravine in the rubble, straight for Janey's neck. She didn't want to kill it, but this was the law of the wild. Kill or be killed. So as the slashing claws of the short front legs moved in above her head, and the creature's exposed underbelly crossed before her eyes, Janey flicked her finger to release the titanium blade and smacked the raptor where she thought its heart must be. The creature screeched and recoiled, falling on top of her, Jane Blonde's Girl-gauntlet buried in its breast. Before it could squash her completely, Alfie drew back his newly Wowed arm and socked the raptor straight across the room with his Boy-battler. They slumped on top of the Wower, panting, as the creature fell silent.

'I don't want to go back that way,' said Janey after a while, pointing to the entry tubes. 'What if it's still alive?'

'I don't THINK so, Blonde,' said Alfie, 'but I know what you mean. Stand back as far as you can.'

Janey watched Alfie punch a hole in the ceiling using the acid-sac in his fist. She just hoped they weren't under the alligator enclosure. There had already been too many tooth-related dangers for one day.

But alligators might have been better than what was actually waiting for them when they clambered up through the hole. Lined up along the wall overlooking the tapir enclosure were some of the scariest creatures Janey had ever seen: three parents, all of whom had been completely – and deliberately – disobeyed.

9 blame for james

They all spoke at once as they pulled Janey and Alfie out of the tapirs' home.

'You've lost James!' cried Janey's mum.

Her father grasped her arm extra tightly. 'You were meant to wait for me, Blonde.'

'Disappointed, Halo,' said Mrs Halliday. 'Very disappointed.'

Janey brushed herself down as she stood up. 'I know, and I'm sorry, but you've got to see what was down there.'

'It's true! There's a dinosaur, large as life and twice as ugly,' said Alfie, miming slashing legs and snapping teeth.

G-Mamma, who had just arrived, ducked down where the tapirs couldn't see her.

'I knew it looked weird!' she hissed, pointing into the enclosure. 'Can it fly?'

Janey looked back at the tapir. It certainly

did look weird, with half its body white and the other half black, and its strange anteater-like nose, but . . . 'G-Mamma, those are tapirs. Zoo animals.'

The SPI:KE got to her feet, assisted by Boz and Alfie. 'I knew that,' she said. 'Tape Ears. Yep, know all about those. So the dinosaur is . . .' She pointed dramatically beneath their feet.

Janey's father held up a hand before anyone else could speak. 'People are staring. Perhaps it would be better if we took this discussion somewhere a little less public. Maisie, would you come with me and help clear up downstairs?'

'The raptor's dead, I think,' said Janey. 'It won't bother you. But the room's a mess.'

'Thank you. You and Alfie take this back to our lab,' said Boz, thrusting a Solfari Lands security video into her hand, 'and your mum and G-Mamma can keep looking for James after you've been dropped off. SPIV us with any info.'

Her mum had saved all her ranting for the drive home, the words floating in and out of Janey's brain as she tried to work out what was going on: '. . . killed . . . how did a dinosaur . . . T. rex and all his friends eating you . . . James might be . . . and after your father specifically *said* . . .'

Where was James? It was quite possible that the raptor had got him before she and Alfie had even reached the Spylab. It was too horrible to contemplate, and yet Janey knew that she had to discover the truth, and quickly – before things got more complicated. Where had the raptor come from? Were there more of them? Were they anything to do with the pelican thing they had seen from the jet? And how did these creatures link to the exploding Spylabs?

'Mum, I'm really sorry,' she said abruptly, interrupting her mum's steady flow of accusations. 'I know we shouldn't have gone against orders and everything, but can you hurry up? This security film might show us where James is, and you can get back to help Dad look for him.'

Jean looked very sternly at her for a moment, then fixed her eyes back on the road. 'You're right, Janey. There are more important things to worry about right now. But don't think you've got away with this. There will be . . . consequences.'

Consequences, thought Janey. What worse consequence could there be than if something had happened to James? She didn't really think sitting in her room thinking about what she'd done was going to help. Sometimes she wished her mum would just stick to spying. Or mothering. But at least make up her mind.

They were home at last. Before the van had pulled up at the gate, Janey had shoved open the door and jumped out, quickly followed by Alfie. 'Bye, Mum,' she called.

'Stay safe, sweetheart!' Jean thrust the car into

reverse. 'And tell one of us the second you find anything out.'

'You too!' Despite the strange politics that had settled on Janey's household, it seemed that everyone was pulling together in the search for James.

They were just reaching the door when the hedge between G-Mamma's house and Janey's shook, and out shot Trouble, eyes bulging with terror, fur stiff with cement dust, haring along as if his life depended on it. He spotted Janey, doubled back and leaped into her arms. Suddenly a dozen small feathered bodies cornered the building like a squadron of tiny fighter jets. 'Told you!' shouted Janey at Alfie, fumbling for the key as twelve sets of teeth looped the loop over the next garden, then zoomed viciously in their direction.

Alfie lifted his hand, still in its Boy-battler, ready to blast down the door, but Janey screamed at him: 'No! If you make a hole in the door, they'll just fly through it.'

With shaking fingers, barely able to see as Trouble scrabbled up her chest and around her neck, she just about managed to turn the key in the lock. Feeling braver from his protected position, Trouble reached out a paw and brandished his claw in the face of the first SParrow. It sped up.

'Incoming!' yelled Alfie. 'Get inside!'

In a flurry of fur they fell through the door, Janey shoving it closed with her foot just as the lead SParrow bared its teeth. Clunk! There was a thump as it hit the wood, then another as it fell to the floor. Janey waited for the other eleven to hit too, but instead there was a furious rasping, cheeping sound, then all went quiet.

Janey shook her head. 'This SParrow power is the last thing we need.' She headed for the kitchen. 'You go to G-Mamma's house to make sure Jamie didn't just come home, and I'll check around here.'

'Spylab in two minutes,' said Alfie, sprinting up the stairs two at a time.

Janey ran through every room, calling for Jamie, and even checked in the garden. The garage doors were firmly locked – there wasn't any way that he could be in there. Disappointed and not a little worried, Janey headed up to the Spylab, where Alfie was already pacing.

'No sign of him,' he said.

'Let's see if this shows us anything,' said Janey, shoving the video into the player.

It showed the security footage from various angles around Solfari Lands. They studied it for several minutes, quickly establishing some SPI entrances and exits: G-Mamma arriving, running after the squawking turkey and giving up at the turnstiles; Trouble at full stretch, with a squadron of little fighter birds after them; Alfie and Janey themselves, turning up with James, talking to each other, and James slipping off among the trees. They scoured the footage from the camera near the

Spylab, watching a small, flitting figure run through the doors barely seconds before the ground rocked . . .

'The explosion,' said Janey.

Alfie paused the tape. 'So James *did* go to the Amphibian House.'

'And probably to the Spylab,' said Janey. 'Remember, he was in that room at the back for a while when he was still a chimp. He must have . . .'

She couldn't bring herself to say it. He had to have been in there when the bomb went off.

'We don't know that,' said Alfie firmly. He hit fast-forward, staring at the figures who milled around in no particular order, looking like puppets. 'Let's try the perimeter fence camera.'

There was nothing until the end of the video, by which time they were practically cross-eyed trying to work out who was where. Then suddenly Janey cried out. 'I saw him! That's Jamie, isn't it?' She pointed to a shadowy form scrambling nimbly up a tree and jumping over the three-metre-high fence that enclosed the whole zoo. 'It has to be him. Only an ex-monkey could shin up a tree that quickly.'

Alfie nodded, peering at the dimly lit vista beyond the perimeter fence. 'Where's he going? There's not much beyond there. Just fields for miles and miles, and then our old school.'

Janey got to her feet. 'Do you think that's where Jamie was heading?'

'Worth a try.'

'We should Wow up properly,' said Janey. Who knew what Jamie was running from? Whatever or who-ever was blowing up Spylabs, she'd rather have the best gear to tackle them.

Moments later, both in their SPIsuits, the two Spylets grabbed an ASPIC each and headed out into the twilight. If they stuck to the back roads, they wouldn't be seen. And if they were, they'd just look like kids out skateboarding, in slightly peculiar outfits.

'Er, weren't you supposed to SPIV your folks?' said Alfie as they skirted the high street and set off across a car park.

Janey felt guilty for about a millisecond, but she truly believed that it was time for Jane Blonde to take control of this mission. 'I don't want to get their hopes up,' she said. 'Let's find him first.'

They were at the school gates now. Checking that nobody was watching, they both pushed one foot down on the back of their ASPICs so the boards stood on their end with the Spylets still suctioned on. Then they slid straight up and over the railings and hit the ground at speed. Swiftly they split up and circled the school, peering into every single window – even the few on the first floor, with the aid of their ASPICs.

'Nothing,' said Alfie.

'Where can he be?' Janey was getting extremely worried. By now it was fully dark, and her brother could be very frightened, alone for so long.

'Oh, Mum must be home,' said Alfie suddenly.

Alfie's house was at the far edge of the school grounds. Sure enough, there were lights on all over the ground floor.

'Or Jamie.'

'Let's go and . . .'

Before Alfie could finish his sentence, there was a strange juddering from the ground beneath them. Both Spylets wobbled on their ASPICs, and Janey stared in horror at Alfie's house. 'Another explosion!' she said. She zoomed in with her Ultra-gogs. 'There's smoke coming from your basement. And . . . Zoom!' She focused on a familiar boyish outline vaulting the fence. 'There's Jamie!'

They both knew what that meant. Another Spylab had just been blown up.

And James was running from the scene of the crime.

10 feathery forests

'Blonde!' An anxious voice blasted up from the SPIV on Janey's chest. 'Update!' shouted her father.

'We're at the Hallidays',' Janey shouted into her own SPI Visualator, swerving around the swings on the school playground as they neared the house. 'There was an explosion, and Jamie was running away.' At the same time Alfie was telling his own mum what was happening.

'We've got it,' said her father. 'Don't go in,' he added sternly. 'Understood?'

Janey paused for a moment, a little sulkily. Judging by his loud 'tut', Alfie had just been told the same thing. 'OK,' she said after a few moments. 'But can I at least go after James?'

'Oh yes!' Her mother's voice rang out. 'She should do that.'

'All right,' said her father, only half his face visible in the screen. It looked like he needed a good shave, and his nose seemed to have spread across his cheeks. 'See if you can track him down. And then straight back to the Spylab at home. We'll rally there at eight p.m.'

'Presuming it's still there,' said Janey.

'We'll double-check,' said her father abruptly. 'Go and find your brother.'

'Right,' said Janey. She swivelled her ASPIC around to face the way James had gone. 'Coming?' she said to Alfie.

To her surprise, he shook his head. 'I'm checking for clues. And making sure my footy cards aren't in little pieces. See you back at the lab.'

Janey nodded. 'Fingers crossed I'll have Jamie with me,' she said, pushing her Ultra-gogs more firmly on to her nose. She knew she had a lot of ground to cover, and quickly – Jamie had bounded over the fence into the woodland surrounding the school. Seized by an idea, Janey headed back to the playground.

At the bottom of the slide she ollied the ASPIC, then hurtled up the mirror-smooth ramp so fast that her ears pressed against the side of her head. She was at the top in less than two seconds; angling her body towards her board like a ski jumper, Janey felt the board part company with the slide. She was flying! The sensation was amazing.

Alfie looked on with a mixed expression, half disgust and half utter admiration. 'Air it, Blonde!' he called back.

Janey loved this feeling of freedom, of sailing through the air. All too soon it was over. After shooting across the fence, clearing it by a good half a metre, Janey pointed the nose of her ASPIC down and headed for the ground. It wouldn't fly forever anyway, as it was more of a hoverboard. With a little bounce the ASPIC made contact with the path at the edge of the woods.

'Night vision,' she said hastily to her Ultra-gogs. In the thick of the trees, she could hardly see. Obligingly her spy glasses switched to active infrared and the objects before her danced up before her eyes in stark black and white. Hovering along a foot above the ground, she was now able to see a grey squirrel running along the branch of a tree, and the bushes moving where something was making them rustle.

Janey slowed and jumped off her ASPIC to investigate. Strapping the board to her thigh, she pushed into the bushes at the place where she spotted the movement. To her disappointment there was nothing odd, only a faint set of marks on the ground where some tiny animal had rushed around in a circle and burrowed under some roots.

Back to the main track she went, looking up from time to time as she ran. The squirrels jumping in and out of the web of branches above her head seemed to be getting more frantic, soaring through the air with their tails and front legs outstretched, flying higher than Janey had on her ASPIC. It was really quite beautiful to watch . . . until two squirrels, in their haste, ran right into each other and toppled to the ground. Landing lightly, cat-like, they stood up for a split second, then pelted away to the safety of a hole in a tree.

'These squirrels are crazy!' Then it suddenly dawned on Janey what she was watching. 'They're being chased.'

Would James be chasing squirrels? She whispered his name a couple of times as loudly as she dared, but there was no reply other than an odd, harsh cawing sound from high above her head.

'Oh no.' The sound was alarmingly familiar, and almost instinctively Janey flicked the titanium blade into position on her Girl-gauntlet. It didn't make sense though. How would the velociraptor, with its lack of balance and its tiny front legs, have managed to climb a tree? Surely she and Alfie had finished him off at Solfari Lands.

There was only one way to find out. Making her way as quietly as she could to a small clearing, Janey pinpointed roughly where the noise was coming from, then jumped. As her soles made contact with the leaf-strewn ground, there were two identical thuds. Her Fleet-feet detonated, and Janey shot upwards. Reaching out, she grabbed hold of a smooth overhanging branch; in one slick movement she swung herself through 360 degrees like a gymnast, then vaulted upwards, landing lightly on top of the branch.

She steadied herself against the trunk, looked around and suddenly spotted the shape she had been searching for. James! He was some way over to her left, huddled under a bush, believing himself to be camouflaged by the undergrowth. His chocolate-button eyes flashed with fear as he peeked out between the leaves, looking in the branches above for whatever had been chasing him.

Following the direction of James's gaze, Janey looked up. The cawing creature was in the tree directly above her head. And it had seen her. Or felt her presence – she wasn't sure which, but she knew from the gasp in the bushes below that James had seen her too, and was fearing for her safety.

'Zoom,' she squeaked to her Ultra-gogs, at the same time holding out a hand towards James and hoping he would understand that he needed to stay quiet.

But when she saw what the spy glasses had focused in on, her heart almost stopped. Unconsciously Janey put a hand over her heart, willing it to be quiet. This time Jane Blonde had surely bitten off more than she could chew.

A glittering eye – cold, tiny and dangerous – was peering down at her. How could it see her through the dark? Too late, Janey noticed the red dot of the active infrared on her Ultra-gogs. She might as well have sat there with a sign over her head saying 'EAT ME'. 'Photo,' she whispered to her Gogs as loudly as she dared. 'And night vision OFF!'

Janey gasped when she saw the photograph taken by the Ultra-gogs: an immense, razor-sharp beak, easily as long as Janey's arm, rounding up to a slight hump below two gimlet eyes, but then extending behind its head like the handle of a sword; a pair of great hunched wings, with one, two . . . three talons that would have matched Trouble's sabre claw for sheer deadliness; long feet that scrabbled uneasily for a foothold in the slender branches at the top of the tree.

What was it? The pelican? It could have followed them from Scotland somehow. It surely couldn't be the velociraptor, but the noise it made was so similar . . .

No time for that now. The creature was getting restless. Crowing ferociously, it reached out one of its three-clawed feet, grappling through the air above her head. It was trying to catch her. Panicking, Janey ran as far as she could along the branch she was on, hoping to be able to leap like a squirrel across to the next tree, but the moment she entered a patch of moonlight the creature stirred excitedly, skimming her ponytail with a claw. She whipped her head around, hoping to knock the monster off balance, but in a matter of moments it had sliced through the platinum strands and was on her again. Now she had no chance . . .

But just as she held out her Girl-gauntlet, ready to

slash through the leathery leg descending through the leaves straight at her, there was a noise below. 'No!' she shouted, horrified.

James had run out from the cover of the bushes. Cupping his mouth, he stood in a shaft of moonlight, fully illuminated, jumping up and down and shouting with his strange voice that sounded so out of practice, still so animal-like. The creature had paused and was listening, watching. The second that he saw he had the creature's attention, James ran, scrambling and scampering over tree roots and low bushes, making as much noise as he possibly could. 'Jamie, no! I can . . .'

But she had dithered, and in that moment the monstrous, ugly bird roused itself from the foliage, unfolded its great sinewy wings and flapped off across the forest. 'Jamie . . .' gasped Janey. 'Not Jamie, please.'

Without taking care to look where she would land Janey leaped from her branch. The ankle that had twinged before now bent at right angles; Janey heard it snap like a dry stick. Her head swam and black mist gathered around her eyes, but somehow her spy instincts prodded her into action. Using her extended titanium blade to slice through the straps of her ASPIC, she flopped full length along it as though it was a surfboard, and with her good foot she pushed off after James, following the path he'd made through the leaves.

She land-surfed through the undergrowth

87

to the edge of the woodland just in time to see her little brother turn and stare, terrified, at the vast bat-like creature bearing down on him. Then it opened its horrendous beak and carried the small boy away like a hawk snatching a mouse.

'Drop him!' screamed Janey, dragging a toe through the dirt to brake and trying to stand up, run, grab her brother's foot. But her ankle gave way, and the last thing she saw before a thick fog dropped down over her eyes was a taloned foot sailing towards the hills . . .

11 compute and dispute

'Blondette, wakey wakey, pale milkshaky.' The familiar voice buzzed over Janey's face in a bothersome fashion. She opened one eye to look at G-Mamma. 'Rise and shine, Spylet mine.'

Sitting up groggily, Janey found her parents, G-Mamma and the Hallidays all peering at her from various parts of the Spylab next to her bedroom, concerned. She was lying on the bed in the corner. Her ankle throbbed gently but had been Wowed, so when she flexed it gingerly it no longer felt broken. 'What happened?' she asked, her tongue feeling too thick for her mouth.

Alfie pointed to the clock, which said 4.45 a.m. 'You didn't arrive at eight, so we sent out a search party.'

'Passed out on the forest floor with ankle pain,' said G-Mamma, mixing something in a glass. 'I think you need a tonic. Drink this.'

'What is it?'

'Melted Mars bars.'

Janey took the glass and, as she sat up, remembered with horrible clarity what had just happened. Or rather, what had happened several hours ago. 'Oh! Jamie . . .'

'He was nowhere to be seen,' said her mother tearfully. 'You didn't find him?'

'I did! He was there in the forest, but there was this thing, this big bat-creature, like that raptor at Solfari Lands, only with wings and a big handle jutting out of its head, and it carried Jamie away, and he looked so scared . . .'

Her father groaned and put his head in his hands. Janey stared. Was she imagining it, or had his hair grown again? It looked coarser, thicker and *blacker* than it had the previous night. She jumped as he sat up and looked straight at her.

'We need a plan of action,' he said firmly, getting up from the bench and pacing and scratching at his arm. 'Halos, you need somewhere to stay for a start, as your house is barely habitable at the moment.'

His glance went from the Hallidays to G-Mamma, who said hotly, 'Look, there's hardly room in the garage to swing a Trouble. I can't be having visitors in there.'

'How bad is your house?' asked Janey.

'Trashed,' said Alfie. 'The Spylab's completely gone, and the rest of the house sort of collapsed into the hole.'

Janey swung her legs over the edge of the bed. 'I . . . I think I might know what's going on,' she said hesitantly. 'That's the third lab now that's been blown up, and we know for definite that Jamie was at Solfari Lands and at the Halos' place. I think maybe he's so mad at what Copernicus did to him, he's smashing up the Spylabs so that Rapid Evolution can't be performed on anyone else.'

The adult SPIs all looked at each other, pondering what she'd said. Then Boz shook his head. 'That may be, Janey, but it doesn't help us find him now, does it? Where do you think this creature was taking him?'

Janey shrugged helplessly. 'Maybe it has a home . . . a whatever you call it that eagles sleep in.'

'An eerie,' said Alfie, looking pleased with himself.

'Yes. Good,' said Boz. 'So here's what we'll do. Hallidays, get some essentials together, and you can have James's room for now, just until we . . . sort things out.' Janey could tell her father was avoiding saying 'until we find him'. 'Gina, you and I should go out beyond the forest and try locating James. G-Mamma, perhaps you could fetch Agent Dubbo Seven across from Oz. We need his tracking skills right now.' He nodded, ticking people off on his fingers.

'What about me?' said Janey.

'Blonde, I need you to do some research,' he said, putting his hands on her shoulders.

91

'Research,' echoed Janey in a hollow voice. She knew what that meant: staying home. Staring at the computer. Missing out on the mission.

Her father nodded urgently. 'Find out whatever you can about these . . . creatures you've been seeing – the biting thing at the zoo, and this monster that carried away your brother . . .'

Well, that was worthwhile, perhaps. 'I'll look them up, find out where they live, where it might have flown to with Jamie, that kind of thing.'

'Alfie can help you when we get back, Janey,' said Mrs Halliday kindly. 'You'll still be feeling a bit muzzy-headed after your blackout.'

'Yeah! She's muzzy. And fuzzy. She's feeling pretty skuzzy,' rapped G-Mamma instantly. 'OK, OK, I'm going,' she finished with a sigh as several people glared at her in unison. Like a dog with a tail between its legs, she slipped downstairs.

One by one they all disappeared after her, until Janey was the only one in the Spylab. As Spylabs seemed to be the target of choice at the moment, she felt a little nervous at being there on her own. 'Trouble,' she called, 'you here? At least if you're here after spying with your freaky collar, I know the place is safe.'

To her relief, the cat strolled out from under the bed, purring madly and rubbing against her legs. All four eyes on his revolting collar pointed towards her at once, the middle two looking distinctly cross-eyed.

Janey shuddered. It looked half alive – it was truly the most hideous creation that G-Mamma had ever come up with. Spinning the collar round so that most of the eyes were out of sight under Trouble's chin, she picked him up and went over to the computer.

First, she typed in 'velociraptor'. Dozens of images of snapping dinosaurs, just like the one she and Alfie had fought, jumped up on to the page before her. 'Dinosaur of the Cretaceous period,' she read aloud. How could a dinosaur be wandering around Solfari Lands? One article in particular caught her eye:

> Scientists say they have evidence that the velociraptor, a dinosaur that lived over 80 million years ago, had a skeleton structure just like modern birds. They found knobs on a fossilized spine that might have been the base of its feathers, which were probably for show, to protect their nests or to keep warm, as the creature didn't fly.

'That's weird,' muttered Janey to Trouble, who cast a sleepy eye in her direction. 'That thing at the zoo was nothing like a bird.'

As for the creature that had carried away James, there was a very simple way to identify it. 'Photo,' she said aloud.

Almost as soon as the word left her mouth, the image of the strange creature popped up on her right lens. Janey took off her Ultra-gogs and downloaded the image to the computer. 'MATCH', she wrote. The computer whirred its way through several million pictures for a few moments. While it was still loading there was a noise downstairs

She tensed, ready for action. Trouble had stiffened too. Janey put a hand on his back to calm him down, but found that his body was vibrating as if an engine was running inside him. 'Trouble, you're purring!' She picked him up.

When a plaintive bleat floated up from the SPIV on her chest, Janey understood. She ran to the top of the stairs; moments later there was a loud hiss and the SPIral staircase capsule slid into place. Out popped G-Mamma and Bert, and scampering ahead of them was Trouble's best friend – a rather moth-eaten sheep with a bald back and great flaps of matted wool hanging around her body like old curtains.

'Maddy!' Janey raced to pet her as Trouble leaped out of her arms and on to the sheep's back, rubbing his head between Maddy's ears. The sheep called 'Paaaaaaaa,' in a tone of utter joy and skittered round the Spylab on her little black hooves, scattering pellets of poo in her wake.

'Stop that, smelly girl,' shouted G-Mamma, narrowly avoiding one as she stepped into the lab.

'G'day, Blonde,' said Bert in his easy drawl. He touched the front of his hat as his leathery face broke into a grin.

Janey gave him a hug. 'It's so lovely to see you! Thanks for coming, Bert. We are totally going to need your help.'

'And where's my huggy-wuggy?' G-Mamma pursed her glittery lips, offended. 'I go right round the world and you don't even say hello? Nobody appreciates me these days.'

Janey giggled and threw her arms as far as they would go around her SPI:KE's waist. 'I do, G-Mamma. But you have only been gone about an hour.'

'And what have you been doing while I was away? Not missing me, obviously,' said G-Mamma with a little sniff.

Janey pointed to the computer screen. 'It's searching for a match for the thing that carried Jamie off. Do you think you'll be able to track it, Bert?'

'I can track any animal known to man,' said Bert with a solemn nod.

But Janey could suddenly see what the match appeared to be. She gulped. This was madness. 'What if,' she said, 'it wasn't known to man?'

They grouped around the computer to see what it was they were dealing with. G-Mamma's mouth fell open, dropping a sticky pineapple cube on to the counter. 'No way, Blonday!'

They all looked again at the word on the screen.

Bert gave a low whistle. 'Well, blow me down,' he said. 'Think I'm gonna need some new tricks for that one.'

12 i am a terror

'Look,' said Bert the morning after James first disappeared, at the spot where he'd been picked up and carried away. 'A few clues, but not enough. First, we know this is where the ptera landed for a moment and picked James up.' Janey had told him this anyway, but he pointed to two roughened patches of earth. 'Pressure release points: these are where James tried to turn to get out of the way of the beak. And this,' he said, indicating a deep ridge in the ground with a couple of small scars on its top edge, 'is where it dug its feet in for a moment while it picked him up. Didn't land for long.'

'I saw it,' said Janey with a nod. 'It just dropped out of the sky and grabbed him, then flew off in that direction, beyond the reservoir.'

Bert squinted at the skyline. 'We could go and check over there for more signs – some sort of trail, or damage, or evidence that it landed. Or . . .' He paused, rubbing his chin.

'Or what?' Alfie stood behind Bert, squinting after him and trying to look rugged.

Bert went on. 'Or we could look for scat.'

'I'll go! What's scat?' Alfie was eager for a job to do.

'Droppings.'

'Oh.' Suddenly he didn't seem quite so keen.

Bert laughed. 'Thing is, I'm not sure I'd recognize pterodactyl droppings even if I fell over them. Not like this,' he said, handing Alfie a tiny hard pellet. 'Squirrel poo.'

'So you'd recognize any other sort of droppings?' said Janey, pocketing the pellet. 'Then all we need to find is some you've never seen before.'

Bert looked at her for a moment, then nodded admiringly. 'Pretty sharp, eh, Blonde?'

'Just another puzzle,' smiled Janey. She'd always been good at working out clues and dingbats, and this really wasn't so different. 'So shall we go?'

'Sure. What's beyond the reservoir?' said Bert. 'Forest?'

'I think so,' said Janey.

But Alfie pulled off his hat and checked his PERSPIRE. 'Not any more,' he said a trifle smugly. 'It's where they're building that new shopping centre.'

Bert shrugged. 'Doesn't matter. Our friend may be long gone anyway by the time we get there. Let's get going, shall we?'

Fleet-footing slowly so as not to miss any potential clues, the three of them made their way across the fields and around the reservoir.

'Here,' said Bert softly. Janey and Alfie crouched down beside him, then followed his pointing finger up through the sparse trees ahead. 'Can you see?'

Janey stared, seeing nothing. Then suddenly she squeaked, 'Yes! I can see where it went!'

She zoomed in with her Ultra-gogs. Several of the trees were crooked at the top, or had broken branches along one side, as if a low-flying aeroplane had brushed along them. 'If we look from broken tree to broken tree,' she said, turning Alfie's head so that he was looking in the right direction, 'we should be able to find the pterodactyl.'

'Or we might at least get a bit of a clue where it's gone,' said Bert, tipping his hat back to wipe his forehead. 'That's what tracking is about – you imagine that there's a rope attached to that ptera, and we're pulling on the end, gathering it in, getting closer and closer.' His voice had dropped to a whisper and the Spylets leaned in, entranced. 'And then, when you get really close, you have to think like that ptera, act like that ptera. You and that creature have to become one. You *are* a ptera.'

'I *am* a ptera,' echoed Alfie, round-eyed.

A shiver ran down Janey's spine as she remembered the empty, glassy stare of the creature, and its vicious beak as it picked up her little brother and carried him away.

Their mood sombre, the three spies set off around the far side of the reservoir. From memory she knew that Sunny Jim's Swims – a former Spylab belonging to Copernicus – lay ahead off to one side and the motorway ran alongside; from the sound of the traffic, it wasn't far away. And on the other side, in what had been rough squares of ploughed earth, the new Winton Mega-Centre was coming to life.

Bert motioned for them to stop. 'See how the ground's getting a bit boggy? We must be getting near one of the feeds for the reservoir.'

'We've got SPIders with us if we want to breathe underwater,' said Janey, not wanting anything to stop them now that they were on James's trail. Suddenly she spotted something.

'Bert!' she hissed. 'Over there on the other side of the motorway – up in that crane.'

'Zoom,' said Alfie and Bert at the same time, staring where Janey was pointing.

'Crikey, you're right, Blonde.'

As quickly as she could, Janey focused her gaze up the neck of the shortest of several cranes to the cage at the top, high above the vast crater in the ground that was due to be a mall in a few years' time. In the corner of the cage was a small patch of maroon and grey. 'It's a Winton United football shirt – James!' Janey could hardly breathe, she was so excited and relieved and worried all at once. 'If we get across the motorway, we can be there in quarter of an hour.'

Even before she'd finished she could see Bert shaking his head. 'No good, Blonde. That big bird is bound to be territorial. If the ptera's in there and we make a heap of noise getting to it, which we'd have to without any equipment and in broad daylight, then he'll just take James somewhere else. And even if he doesn't, then James will be in more danger – that thing won't leave him alive if he thinks we're going to try to nab him.'

'But then what are we going to do? How are we supposed to get to him silently? Even Maddy beats her wings and makes a noise . . .'

But then Bert's words raced through her mind and she stood still, thinking: you must *become* the ptero-dactyl, you *are* the pterodactyl.

Well, perhaps she couldn't be the pterodactyl, but she was pretty sure she could be something like the creatures she'd seen flying above her head, sailing through the trees, avoiding its grasp . . .

And suddenly she was off, Fleet-footing at speed around the reservoir in the direction of the town, Alfie and Bert huffing as they struggled to keep up with her. 'I don't understand,' said Alfie as they crested the hill. 'Have you just given up?'

'No way,' said Janey, taking the slope down at a run. 'I'm going to see G-Mamma. She needs to make me something. Pronto!'

secret squirrel

'I don't know how,' said Janey to the back of G-Mamma's head as the SPI:KE did press-ups on the garage floor, 'but whatever you did to combine those eyes with Trouble's collar, and those birds with arrows to make the SParrows, you can do the same with this squirrel dropping, can't you?'

G-Mamma collapsed in a heap in her straining Lycra gym gear, panting heavily. 'Birds and arrows? What are you on about?'

'Those vampire sparrows that were chasing you and Trouble down the street.'

'Nothing to do with me,' said G-Mamma, heaving herself into a sitting position, roly-poly and floppy as a Cabbage Patch doll. Hmm, thought Janey – doubt-ful! 'But here's something I did make!' she added brightly, handing Janey a pair of furry ear-phones, one black and one white. 'You gave me the idea at the zoo. These are Tape-Ears. Like an old-fashioned cassette tape – press the black one and it records your conversations.'

Janey put them on hesitantly, then found the knobble on the earpiece to press. Sure enough, a slight whirring sound in her left ear suggested that whatever she and G-Mamma said next would be recorded. 'Very useful,' she said tactfully, although she wasn't sure anything so big and obvious would be much use in the world of Solomon's Polifical Investigations. 'What does this one do – AAARGH!'

She yanked the headphones off, clutching her head in pain. G-Mamma's rapping in her right ear had been astonishingly loud, even though the words were . . . well, more like a love song. Janey could still hear it now, echoing in a tinny fashion off the metallic floor of the garage. *I was all you were needing; now my heart, it's all bleeding . . . Dripping on to the floor; just can't take any more . . .*

G-Mamma leaped across the room and grabbed the Tape-Ears in a sliding tackle. 'Don't . . . that's . . . the right ear's just a docking station for my MP3.'

'So who was that?' asked Janey suspiciously.

'Oh, that new band, you know, with Gwen Wotsername, and . . . um . . . OK, fine, girl-spy. Just shine a light in my eyes and have done with it, why don't you?' huffed G-Mamma. 'I admit it. It's me. I've done a demo tape, if you must know.' She slid aside the mirrored door to the left of the fridge to reveal a whole bank of music equipment. 'And all those press-ups were to get fit for my music video. Bert's going to shoot it for me.'

Janey could not think of a single thing to say that would be the right response. 'Great!' was all she could manage. Nodding blankly, she picked up the squirrel dropping again. 'And speaking of Bert reminds me. Can you use this to make me fly like a squirrel?'

'I'll give it a go,' said G-Mamma, looking very pink and rather glad to change the subject. 'It's an advanced programme on the Wower that I've been experimenting with.'

Opening the door to the Wower, the SPI:KE ushered Janey inside and then lobbed the squirrel pellet in after her. Janey caught it just as the door shut and G-Mamma yelled, 'Wow and WELD.'

'G-Mamma, why do I . . .'

It was too late. Janey glanced around nervously as a metal hand reached for the back of her head. Not for a moment had she imagined that she would have to be transformed herself, just for a new outfit to be created. She thought about the horrible eyes on Trouble's collar and shuddered. It was quite possible she would step out of the Wower like some kind of mutant squirrel, maybe with huge front teeth, or a great bushy tail . . .

Meanwhile, rather to her disgust, a thin probe snaked out of the Wower wall and grabbed the poo pellet from her hand; as her head was massaged and her Ultra-gogs slid into place, the probe rubbed the pellet up and down her arms and legs. 'Euw! Don't! What are you doing?'

As quickly as it had appeared, the probe shot back into the wall, taking what was left of the squirrel dropping with it. She could feel her body being encased in her Lycra SPIsuit, just as normal.

A moment later the lights flashed around the Wower. 'Wow and Weld complete,' said a smooth female voice. 'Jane Blonde, you may exit the cubicle and begin your next mission.'

'Thank you,' said Janey, although why she was thanking a machine she wasn't quite sure. There was something about that voice though . . .

'Jane Blonde.' Suddenly it started up again. 'You've mixed it. Now exit. It's really . . . your time. Aha: you've mixed it. Now max it, you Spylet . . . divine.'

So G-Mamma had reprogrammed lots of things about the Wower. Janey smiled.

'Looking good,' said G-Mamma, now wrapped in a white dressing gown and kick-boxing a punchbag that hung over the old tyre in the corner. 'How is that for you, Secret Squirrel?'

Janey looked down, then gasped. Turning around slowly, she stared at her reflection in the Wower door. 'I *am* a ptera,' she said.

'You are a terror?' said G-Mamma.

'No, I mean – I'm like a pterodactyl.'

Her SPIsuit was as silver and tight-fitting as ever, and her feet were encased in familiar aerodynamic Fleet-feet. Between her arm and leg on each side, however, there was now a flap of dark grey, shimmering material forming a triangle along either side; if she'd had claws on her elbows, Janey could have done a very good imitation of the crouching pterodactyl. A similar piece of fabric joined her legs together, wide enough at the bottom that she could still stretch her feet far apart. Janey did a star-jump and laughed. She looked like a kite. And it occurred to her that that was just the point. She was going to be able to free-fall silently in this suit, not disturbing the ptera, as she flew in to rescue James.

G-Mamma came up behind her and tapped the large lump between her shoulder blades. 'This is a parachute for when you've been free-falling for long enough and you're nearer the ground. Your helmet is shaped to cut through the wind like a racing cyclist,' she said, rapping the top of Janey's head sharply. The helmet jutted out front and back into a sharp point, rather like the pterodactyl's head, but with a small microphone attached near the chin strap. Beneath the back of the helmet sat her bushier-than-usual ponytail, curving to a sleek platinum curl at the end. 'Like a squirrel's tail,' said Janey, flicking it this way and that.

'It should help you steer,' said G-Mamma.

107

'Their pretty, fluffy tails aren't just for show, you know.'

Janey peeked through the window. 'Well, it's dark now. I'm ready to go.'

As she spoke there was a ferocious mewling from inside the Wower.

'Trouble! How did you get in there?' Janey threw open the door and grabbed her cat, holding him up above her head as she studied what the Wower and pellet had done to him. His back legs were webbed, and his golden tail was bigger and bushier than ever. Trouble miaowed happily, revealing two long front teeth. 'You've turned into a fat tabby squirrel! I suppose you'd better come with me then.'

G-Mamma stopped her at the door. 'Small question, Blondette. How the squirrelly squirts are you planning on getting up to the top of that crane?'

'Well, I do have one idea . . .'

'My little fighter jet?' G-Mamma blinked innocently.

Janey stared. 'You brought that fighter jet home out of the moat? Where is it?'

'Out there,' said G-Mamma, pointing to the allotment across the gravel road. Janey peered through the grimy window. There did seem to be a strange shape buried under a mountain of net, which the turkeys were pecking at disconsolately. 'That's how that turkey got out.'

'The jet would be brilliant,' said Janey, trying not to laugh, 'but Bert says I have to get up there silently. So here goes.'

Janey opened the door, whistled softly and in trotted Maddy the sheep, followed by Bert and then her parents. Janey stopped short, feeling as if she'd been caught doing something wrong.

'Al Halo told me before he left that you're going after this pterodactyl,' said her father, his voice as dark as the five o'clock shadow sweeping his chin. 'When exactly were you planning on telling us?'

Janey looked at the floor. 'Um . . . afterwards?'

'I'm sure Janey had her reasons for keeping it to herself,' said her mum, laying a hand on Boz's arm as if to calm him. 'You do have reasons, don't you?'

'Yes,' said Janey confidently. 'Number one, James is stuck out there for a second night on his own, and we need to get to him quickly. Two, of everybody he knows, he's least scared of me – the last thing we need him to do is panic. And three . . . I'm the lightest and can skydive down to him without disturbing the ptera.'

Her father looked over at Bert. 'Don't blame me,' said Bert, holding up his spade-like hands. 'It was all her own idea. Pretty darn clever though, if you ask me.'

'We can all go with her to the launch site,' said Janey's mum. 'Then James will have us there for him if – I mean when – he's rescued.'

Boz looked from one to the other of them, thinking hard, raking through the coarse hair on the back of one hand with the fingers of the other. His hand? Janey sneaked another glance at him. It was true; the backs of both hands were distinctly hairy. 'Fine,' said Boz at length. 'Blonde it is. I see you're all ready to go.'

'I just need my transport now,' said Janey, inwardly breathing a sigh of relief.

And, as she'd hoped, Maddy the special sheep needed no second bidding. She loved being a little aeroplane, just as she had when she'd taken on Copernicus and the SPIclone in her home at Dubbo Seven. As soon as the Wower door opened she pelted inside, and when her bleat changed from her usual 'paaaaaa' to a smooth growl like the engine of G-Mamma's Pet Jet but a million times quieter, Janey let her out into the Spylab again. The Wowed sheep emerged at eye level, hovering gently on the angel wings that had sprung from her sides in place of the flaps of knotty wool. She dropped down so that Janey could climb on to her back, but Janey shook her head. 'You need to save your strength, Maddy,' she said. 'Let's wait until we get near the building site.'

On the way to the launch site, Maddy sat with Trouble in the back of the Clean Jean van. Crowded into the front seats were Janey and her parents, while G-Mamma and Bert powered along behind on a couple of industrial mops the size of dustbin lids, motorized to become Segways, or SPISegs, as Bert had christened them.

'Mmmm, Spice Eggs, now they sound ni-i-ice,' said G-Mamma, straddling the mop handle. 'Spice Eggs, those nice eggs, they're tasty and true . . .'

'Focus, Rosie,' said Bert softly. 'It's a SPI-Seg. SPI pause Seg. Repeat after me.'

'Oh, shut up. Always spoiling my fun,' grumbled G-Mamma, but she didn't really sound very mad about it. Riding on the solid disk that had once been the mop head, G-Mamma dared to take her hand off the stick just long enough to give Janey a thumbs-up through the back windscreen. She wobbled, shrieked and quickly grabbed hold of the handle again.

Like an all-terrain vehicle – Janey suspected Bert had been tinkering with more than just the mops – the Clean Jean van traversed rough land around the reservoir and followed one of the tributaries under the motorway through thirty centimetres of water, dodging tree trunks and foliage. As soon as Janey saw one of the cranes through her Ultra-gogs she tapped her mum on the shoulder. 'I think we should stop here and walk the rest of the way. We don't want the pterodactyl to hear us.'

The others agreed, and before too long the group was forging its way through the undergrowth to the edge of the area quarried for building. One by one, as they reached the designated spot for launching, the

III

SPIs all zoomed in with their Ultra-gogs. 'Don't put your active infrared night vision on,' warned Janey.

'Thermal imaging then,' said Boz, and the spy glasses obediently switched to heat-seeking vision. Immediately two things became clear: James was definitely in the cage, cowering or crouching in a corner; and the pterodactyl was flying around just above, guarding its prey.

'James must hate that,' said Janey. 'I bet it reminds him of . . . you know, his other cage.'

'It's now or never,' said G-Mamma, straightening Janey's ponytail. 'Go to it, Blondette.'

'And be careful! Here, give me a hug.' Janey's mum grabbed her quickly and squeezed very hard, and for a moment Janey recalled life before all this had happened, when her mum's hugs had meant everything to her. She gave her a kiss on the cheek and turned to her father to hug him, but somehow she ended up colliding awkwardly with his ear.

'Sorry, darling,' he said in his unusually gravelly whisper. 'Good luck, Blonde. Bring our boy home.'

'I will,' she said solemnly. 'Trouble, Maddy – let's go.'

And a few minutes later, with only a shaft of weak moonlight indicating the way to go, a flying sheep flung itself off the edge of a crater and pushed on up through the darkness, with a Spylet in a squirrel suit and a half-mutated cat hanging on to its back for dear life.

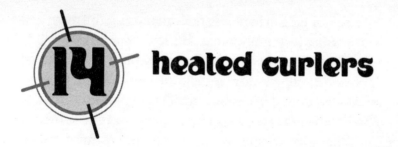

heated curlers

Maddy's flight was eerily quiet – just a barely audible hum and the gentle swoosh of her white wings breaking the silence. Janey kept the cave and the pterodactyl in her sights on the Ultra-gogs, steering Maddy in the direction of the little red blob on the tiny screen, and the bigger red blob swooping menacingly above it. Trouble crouched between Janey's knees, his great golden tail now so enormous and bushy that it tickled her chin. Janey pulled back on Maddy's ears so they all rose higher into the night sky.

The pterodactyl was flitting between the tops of two cranes, seeming to move so slowly and deliberately that it looked as though it was hanging in mid-air. Janey swallowed, a little nervous. The closer they got, the bigger the creature looked, and the more vulnerable little James appeared, swinging dangerously in the wired top of the crane.

'OK, team,' she whispered to her spy-pets.

'We're going to have to distract that thing for me to get close enough to grab Jamie. Can you do that?'

Trouble arched his back, preening. No doubt that he could do it. Maddy just let out the tiniest of 'paaas', in what sounded like a confident sheep voice. 'Up then, Maddy, please. We need to get above old Ptera there.'

She was trusting her safety and James's to an untested squirrel suit, but as there didn't really seem to be much choice she put that thought out of her mind. 'Here we go,' she hissed, as Maddy hovered above the menacing, spiky shape of the pterodactyl. 'On three – I'll go this way –' she pointed – 'and you two go that way.'

This is all a bit mad, she thought as she carefully got to her feet on Maddy's polished rounded seat. She'd soon find out whether the suit worked. After a few moments to steady herself, she stood up and stretched out her arms. Instantly the wind filled the sails beneath her arms and she swayed back and forth, staggering to keep her footing on Maddy's back. It's now or never, Blonde, she told herself sternly. 'One . . . two . . . THREE!'

She launched herself up and out against the backdrop of cranes, mechanical equipment and half-built megastores against the starry sky, her profile in the shadows identical to the prehistoric creature she was chasing. She flew up and back, caught by the wind that made the arm-sails and the flap between her feet billow and snap. For a moment she spun, fearing she was going to drop, and then suddenly she stretched her arms out and found some kind of jet stream. The next instant she was soaring, swooping, skydiving, angling her body this way and that to catch the eddies that were holding her up, the wind whistling across the dome of her helmet. 'This is superb!' she cried, forgetting for a moment that she was on a mission.

Too late. The pterodactyl had heard her. It cocked its head, a beady eye penetrating the darkness. Confused, the creature flapped up towards her, then turned and headed back towards the cage. 'No!' screamed Janey. That was the last thing she wanted. She could really only 'fly' downwards; if the dino-bird took off across the hills with James in its jaws, she wouldn't be able to follow.

Her scream worked, and the bird-like monster whipped its bony head around to find her. 'Oops.' Now it had a very clear idea where she was. With a beat of its leathery wing, the pterodactyl turned and headed straight for her.

'Trouble . . . Maddy . . .' shouted Janey, scanning the skies for the sheep as she was buffeted this way and that by the turbulence. 'Decoy!'

Suddenly the pterodactyl gave one of its harsh cries and bent around. Janey zoomed in and saw something dripping from its feet – blood? There was only one thing that could have slashed it in mid-air . . .

She caught sight of Maddy overhead – at the sound of the Spylet's call the sheep must have veered around and dropped Trouble into the fray. He hung in a thermal, taunting the pterodactyl away from Janey. The sabre claw that had just sliced through the creature's skin winked in the moonlight, but even that was overshadowed by the sheer glory of Trouble's golden tail. Fluffed out by the wind, it was the same size as the rest of his body. He looked rather like a flying cushion.

The cat attack was more than enough to distract the pteradactyl. Squawking, it angled its massive beak towards Trouble and dived. Trouble let out a shrill miaow – whether through fear or excitement, Janey couldn't tell. He tumbled for several metres, the creature snapping at his rear end, then suddenly Trouble found a current of air. He was off, whipping through the air, this way and that, confusing the pterodactyl by seeming to fall within its grasp and then whisking out of reach.

Janey spun around in an eddy of wind. The creature was getting angrier and angrier, carving through the air with its ferocious talons. Trouble had done his job well. And just as it looked as though the ptera might get close enough to do Janey some damage, there was an outraged 'paaaaaaa' from above, and the creature found itself dive-bombed by a flying sheep.

It was time for Blonde to make her move. 'Spylet Sable,' yelled Janey, wishing there was some other way she could get his attention, 'I'm coming to get you. Stand up.'

As she dived she focused on James through her Ultra-gogs, and within moments she was approaching the top of the crane.

There was a problem though. Rather a large one. 'I don't know how to stop!' squeaked Janey as the metal surface hurtled up to meet her. If she carried on like this she would smack into it at about 150 miles an hour, and then there would be nothing left of her to save James or anyone else with, ever again. Alarmed, she rolled her right arm around so that she changed direction, away from the crane. James let out a small cry.

'Don't worry!' she shouted. 'I'm coming back.'

But just as she spun back towards the cave in a rather clumsy circle, her nylon wings rattling like the fuselage of a plane, she felt a searing pain through her ankle – the same ankle that had failed her in the woods. She looked down. 'No!' She was being dragged. The pterodactyl had her by the foot and was pulling her back towards the crane. Now after having James for a main meal, the monster could eat her for dessert.

'It's got me,' she gasped into her microphone. Perhaps her parents or G-Mamma could do something. She coursed through the air, trying to kick at the creature but managing instead to drive its beak through the tightly woven material stretched between her feet. There was a horrible ripping sound, then Janey dropped backwards. Now she was dangling helplessly by the foot, with no more strength than a rag doll, from the mouth of the pterodactyl. James's anxious face was getting ever nearer. Very soon she would be joining him in the cage . . .

Maddy took charge. Flying below Trouble so that she could scoop him up on to her back, she winged her way from the nearby crane and – *boof!* The sheep slammed into the side of the ptera. In the same instant, Trouble jumped off her back and wound himself, mewling and scratching, around the leathery neck of the monster. With an outraged caw it released its grip on Janey's ankle and she plummeted towards the ground. She had no wings beneath her feet. She was going to die anyway . . .

Trouble and the pterodactyl tumbled through the air, head over vicious feet. As Trouble lashed out with his sabre claw, catching the ptera across the eye, Maddy swooped around and flew just over Janey's head. Gratefully seizing a little cloven hoof, Janey watched as Trouble pushed off the dino-bird and streamed across the sky, leaving a red trail behind him. What *was* that? Janey focused more clearly on Trouble. Fire? Yes! It was coming from his tail. Trouble's fluffy golden fur was alight, and the flames were enormous.

'Maddy, take me up to James,' called Janey.

With a bit of difficulty the pair flew above the

crane and Janey dropped into position, still trying to keep one eye on her Spycat. With a painful crunch she hit the metallic arm of the crane. For a moment she thought she might tumble off, but her magnetic Fleet-feet pinged into action. She clung on like a crab, scuttling sideways up the mile-high metal slope towards the cage. Seconds later, she had sawn her way in.

'Jamie!' she said, wrapping her winged arms around her little brother. 'You've had us all worried to death.'

James blinked solemnly, then pointed out into the night sky.

'I know. Trouble's in . . . trouble,' said Janey.

The cat was streaking through the sky like a comet, but the pterodactyl was obviously able to detect heat as well as light. Furious, nipping at its own feet to stop the flow of blood, it sped after Trouble with only one thing on its mind. And even though Maddy was flying along after him, she wasn't fast enough to catch up. All three of them could only look on helplessly as the dino-bird gained on Trouble and opened its jaws.

It was even more horrible than Janey could ever have imagined. As the hideous beak clamped around Trouble's tail, it came off in the pterodactyl's mouth. The cat turned, yowling, but then stopped short, stunned into silence by the sight of his beautiful tail parting company from his bottom. With a cry the creature dropped the great plume and

swooped back round, but Trouble, with no tail to follow – or to hold him up – had disappeared from view.

Maddy fluttered nearby for a moment, then
zoomed off to find her friend, bleating pitifully.

'No . . .' Janey gathered James to her side, block-
ing his view, hardly able to comprehend what she had
just seen. Her beloved Spycat had been ripped apart
before her eyes, dying just to save her, and she still
hadn't even managed to do what she had set out to
on her mission. James – and now Blonde – were both
captive in the cage, with the dino-bird winging its way
back towards them.

And suddenly, instead of being upset, Janey found
that she was furious. 'You do NOT kill my Spycat,' she
roared. 'You evil . . . horrible . . . aaarggh!'

Grabbing James's hand, she ran back and forth
in the cage, until she'd tipped it by forty-five degrees,
then she launched herself off the top of the crane.
The squirrel suit picked up enough wind in its wings
to allow her to hover for a few moments. But James
weighed her down. And her suit had been ripped.
She probably had about five seconds before they both
plunged to their deaths.

Well, that wasn't going to happen, she decided.
'Come on then, you big chicken,' she yelled at the pterodactyl, unbuckling the SuSPInder from her waist.

As the creature swooped, Janey swung. The next
second, the pterodactyl found itself lassoed by a string

of steel loops, with Janey and James swinging on the end. The weight made it drop; as it plummeted across the motorway towards the reservoir Janey called out to James, 'We're going to swing back and then . . . JUMP!'

Together they allowed the drag to pull them backwards. Then, just as they reached the trees near the reservoir, Janey let go of James's hand so that he fell to the ground, landing lightly among the leaves. He watched, bewildered, as she swung past on the end of the SuSPInder, but she smiled reassuringly. 'Just wait there.'

The pterodactyl tried to lift itself above the trees. As Janey's legs made contact with the treetops, she made sure her Girl-gauntlet had the tightest grip possible on the SuSPInder. Then she wrapped her legs around the top of a tree trunk, and pulled. The dino-bird squawked furiously and tried to yank itself away, but in vain. Janey wrapped her end of the SuSPInder firmly around the trunk and then she let go and climbed down the tree.

The four SPIs had run to find them; James was being crushed in a hug from Janey's mum, although he was staring over her shoulder at Janey's dad in awe. Boz did look odd, thought Janey, and when she peered more closely she realized why. He was much more hairy than before in general, but now his eyebrows had joined together in the middle like a furry centipede, his whole forehead seeming to bulge.

Janey tore her eyes away. 'The pterodactyl's tethered at the top of the tree. Thought you might want to look at it,' she said, and Bert hurried past her to get it.

'And Trouble . . . is . . .'

She couldn't even say the word, and one look at G-Mamma's blue eyes swimming with tears was enough to make her sob herself. What was going on with the world? Trouble gone. Weird creatures chasing them around the forest. And her father turning into what looked like . . . a werewolf.

 **trouble's tale**

Tap tap scrape. Tap tap scrape.

Having tossed and turned all through the rest of the night, Janey was roused from an uncomfortable slumber by a tapping sound. At first she wondered if she was still dreaming; the noise sounded very like the banging at the back of the fireplace that had first alerted her to G-Mamma's spy world all those months ago. But this sound was coming from the window and was quickly followed by a loud 'OW!' and then a stifled shriek.

Janey raced to the window. In the dim dawn light she could see G-Mamma lying in the flower bed, a short upside-down stepladder half buried in the dirt next to her. The SPI:KE was swatting at one of the vampire sparrows, which was buzzing around her head. She struggled to her feet, wiping clumps of mud from her black outfit. It was flowing and floor length, and she had topped it off with a tight black skullcap with chiffon sides and back hanging over her curls. Like a mad nun, thought Janey.

'I was just up the Bladder here, trying to wake you up, when one of those vampire sparrows attacked me. They're . . . OUCH . . . Murdery birdery, there's more of them! Meet me in my Spylab!' Hoiking her skirts above her black wellington boots, G-Mamma ran for the garage, her flowing headdress pecked at by the flesh-eating birds of her own creation.

It sounded urgent. Maybe the others were already down there. Not bothering to change out of her pyjamas, Janey scurried down the stairs and ran out of the back door towards the garage.

But to her surprise G-Mamma was alone in the garage-cum-Spylab. Checking furtively over Janey's shoulder, the SPI:KE ushered her in to a lab that looked more like one operated by Copernicus than a member of SPI. Every surface had been shrouded with shimmering black material, and projected on to the fridge was a video showing Trouble in various poses: Trouble as a kitten, running away from a mouse; Trouble draped around G-Mamma's neck like a fox-fur; Trouble Wowed into the squirrel shape only the previous night . . .

Janey's eyes filled up. 'Poor Trouble,' she said.

'I thought we should have a little fu . . . funer . . . ceremony,' gulped G-Mamma, pausing to blow her nose on a black silk handkerchief the size of a pillowcase. 'You know what I mean.'

'Should we invite the others?'

'No,' said G-Mamma with considerable feeling. 'Nobody else appreciated him the way that you and I do, Blonde. I mean, did.'

'I think Dad did,' said Janey, but even as she said it she realized that this was possibly not true any more. Her father was changing, becoming more and more angry and short with her, and more and more, well, hairy, and lumpy in the face.

G-Mamma had already turned away to the work-bench, fiddling with her Tape-Ears which had both been draped in black in honour of the occasion. A loud drone filled the room. 'Bagpipes,' said G-Mamma with a sniff. 'He always loved bagpipes.'

Janey patted her arm, feeling so miserable, so lost without her cat that she could barely look at the little box G-Mamma had filled with his favourite things – a bottle of water, the Spyroscope that used to hang like a bell from his collar, and a photo of him with his Elvis quiff and his bright golden tail. 'He was so proud of that tail,' she whispered.

Suddenly G-Mamma burst into song, in a hideous nasal screech that was even worse than the bagpipes:

> 'Trouble, oh Trouble, you cat of the sky.
> Now you're in Heaven, though Heaven knows
>   why . . .
> Trouble, dear Trouble, oh Spycat supreme,

125

*We know that, in kitty clouds, your tail's
        all . . . a-gleam.'*

With her chins wobbling furiously, the SPI:KE picked
up the lid of the cardboard box and placed it cere-
moniously on the top. Then, enveloping Janey in a
shuddering hug, she whispered, 'I'll bury it later, when
it's dark, as we've no actual . . . you know.'

Janey wiped a tear from G-Mamma's black veil.
No actual *body*, was what G-Mamma was avoiding
saying. No body, and no tail. The bridge of her nose
burned painfully as she fought back her tears. Burned
like his poor tail, she thought. Why *had* his tail been
burning?

And with the bright flash in her brain that accompanied her best ideas, Janey thought of something. She
scooted over to the computer and keyed in 'Squirrel's
tails'.

'What are you doing?' howled G-Mamma. 'It's
Trouble's fu . . . fu . . . special party! It's not the time
to be typing.'

Janey mustn't get G-Mamma's hopes up. She
shouldn't get her own hopes up, she realized, but if
there was the faintest chance that Trouble's tail had
come off by design rather than by accident, then there
was also the hope that he wasn't actually dead. 'I'm just
writing a letter – to go in his special box,' she said, staring anxiously at the computer screen.

At that G-Mamma threw herself across her make-up bench, wailing pitifully. 'Oh, he'll never look at me with those big green eyes again. Oh, I can't bear it. Kill me, Blonde, kill me too! I'll join him on his little cat cloud in the sky . . .'

'You may not have to,' said Janey under her breath. An article had popped up on the screen before her.

It was better than she had ever dared to hope.

The Squirrel's Tale
How the squirrel uses its tail to divert danger

Scientists have discovered that squirrels may have the most useful tail of all animals. Not only does it heat up and swell in size, to scare off predators like snakes and burn them if they do still attack . . .

Yes! thought Janey. She read on eagerly.

. . . but it now appears they could have another ace up their furry sleeve. Like certain breeds of lizard, the squirrel may have the ability to shed its tail when under attack, leaving it free to escape up the nearest tree, completely unharmed.'

'G-Mamma,' she said, feeling a little breathless, 'when Trouble Wowed up with that pellet, how much of him was actual *squirrel*, do you think?'

G-Mamma lifted her head from the bench,

mascara in thick black brushstrokes across her cheek. 'I don't know, Blonde. What a time to be asking things like that. He was all cat to me.'

'But I don't think he was,' said Janey. 'If he was, say, half-squirrel, then I think . . .' She hardly dared to believe it herself. '. . . I think he might be alive.'

She pointed to the computer screen, and G-Mamma skidded across the room towards her. 'Blonde, how could he . . . ? Oh, his tail might have . . . but how could he . . . ?'

Janey raced for the Wower. 'I'm going to find out,' she said. 'He might still be in the woods near the reservoir, in pain, wondering why nobody's come to rescue him. Though Maddy went that way too. Is she home? Get Bert – he can help us!' she yelled as the Wower door closed behind her.

She felt a lot better as the Wower worked its magic, replacing her wrinkled, sweat-dampened pyjamas with smooth silver Lycra and smoothing her tousled hair into her trademark ponytail of sleek platinum blonde. It even seemed to be helping her to think more clearly, and as the droplets shimmered and glittered around her she came to a few decisions, marking them off in the steamed glass surrounding her.

1. Dad
There was definitely something not right about her father. He was getting more dangerous-looking and

more crotchety by the day. He barely grunted at her. Was he ill? Did he know something that they didn't? Had he been experimenting again – on himself, as he always did first? She intended to find out.

2. James
Why did he run off like that in the first place? Wasn't he happy? Was he escaping something? And did he have anything to do with the explosions?

3. Spylabs
WHO WAS BLOWING THEM UP? AND WHY?

4. Creatures
Pterodactyls. Velociraptors. How had these strange animals from the past ended up in Winton? How were they even alive?

As the steam evaporated and her Wower came to an end, Jane Blonde stepped out into the Spylab, bursting with curiosity and ready for action. It was time to sort a few things out. Beginning with . . .

'Trouble,' she said firmly.

129

sunny jim's swims

Janey had forgotten, however, that it was now a new day, and that the family would be gathering for breakfast. The first thing she saw when she walked out of the garage was the sunlight, and the second was her mum standing on their back doorstep, her arms folded and her expression rather stony.

'We are meant to be in this together, Janey,' she said in a very disapproving voice. Janey noticed that she was wearing her bronze SPIsuit under her dressing gown, while her hair was gleaming like a bronze motorcycle helmet. 'G-Mamma says you think Trouble might be alive.'

Janey nodded, peering past her mum to see her father, hunched over his cereal, and James, picking listlessly at a bunch of grapes. 'I was just going to go and look for him myself,' she said. 'Didn't want to get everyone's hopes up . . . just in case.'

Nobody could argue with that. Her mum nodded

sympathetically, and they went indoors together. 'Our Blonde wants to go and find Trouble,' said her mum. 'There's no problem with that, is there?'

Boz glanced up from beneath his mono-brow, and Janey felt even her mother flinch beside her. 'No,' he growled. 'Take Sable.'

'What about Bert? He'd be useful for tracking,' said Janey.

'He and G-Mamma have gone to take the ptera to the zoo. They'll meet you in the forest, where you saw Trouble drop. And jeans over your SPIsuits,' she added. 'It's broad daylight. You never know who you might bump into.'

Once they were in their ordinary clothes Boz drove Janey and James close to the point where the pterodactyl chase had begun. He was obviously brooding over some problem or other; every so often he shot one of them a hunted look. For a moment, Janey even felt sorry for him.

'Are you OK?' she said. 'You know you can talk to me, your ace Spylet.'

But Boz simply grunted and then pointed out of the window. The tree where the pterodactyl had been tethered was just a few metres away. It was a good place to start tracking. 'One o'clock – back here,' growled Boz as they climbed out of the Clean Jean van.

That gave them just under three hours. Janey nodded and took her little brother's trembling hand.

'Don't worry,' she said. 'The monster's all tied up at Solfari Lands. It won't bother you again.'

She hoped not, at any rate, though at this point there was no telling what other creatures might be lurking in the forest. Pushing back the brim of her baseball cap, Janey focused with her Ultra-gogs. 'X marks the spot,' she said. The map of the area had a large cross on it about four kilometres away – the place where they believed Trouble, or what was left of him, had fallen out of the sky. 'Come on, Sable.'

Together they ran, their Fleet-feet enabling them to cover the distance in less than ten minutes. As they got nearer the site, the locator on Janey's spy glasses started to beep at exactly the same moment that James started to gibber excitedly. 'Well done,' said Janey admiringly. Her brother's animal instincts were as finely tuned as her Ultra-gogs. 'So, what are we looking for . . .'

Jamie put his hands together in a time-out sign, followed by a crooked finger in his left palm.

'T . . . R . . .' spelled Janey. 'Oh! Trouble. Yes, we are searching for him, but we're also looking for signs of where he might be if he's hiding, or hurt.'

Giving her the OK sign, James dropped to his knees and started foraging around in the leaves, checking particularly under bushes. Janey moved out in a wider circle, using her Ultra-gogs to step in where her human senses might not be strong enough. 'Heat sensor, DNA check on fur or . . . or blood, and print magnification,' she instructed her glasses. They flickered before her eyes for a moment, and she worried that she had confused them with too many orders at once, but suddenly the picture cleared.

'James!' she cried. 'Over here.'

It was part of Trouble's Cat's Eye Collar – specifically, an eye. Blue and long-lashed, it stared up from the ground like a painted pebble. Janey picked it up gingerly. The Wow and Weld did a spectacular job. Spectacular, but not always pleasant. 'Euw,' she said. 'It's warm. But it's definitely off Trouble's collar! This must be where he fell.'

But of Trouble himself there was no sign. They were moving closer to the reservoir, and the ground underfoot was becoming muddy. 'Trouble loves water,' said Janey, trying to think logically. 'If he thought he was on fire he would have headed here, tried to swim to safety.'

James simply nodded, then cried out. He was pointing to the ground.

'Tracks,' whispered Janey.

She knew without checking that they were Trouble's prints. Rather on the large side for cat paws, there was a slash in the mud in front of the print from the left front leg. His sabre claw. 'He was going this way,' she said. 'And look.'

On either side of the cat prints were other sets of

prints. One was completely identifiable – human feet. Large ones. Shod in heavy boots, by the looks of it. 'Bert's, I bet,' she said, her Ultra-gogs confirming that the boots were an Australian brand. 'Looks like he's found Trouble! But what are these?'

The markings in the ground to the other side of Trouble's prints were not ones Janey recognized. There were four rectangular indentations, quite evenly spaced, each a good ten centimetres deep. 'That's either a very funny animal,' said Janey, as she and James pored over the tracks, 'or someone brought a piece of furniture out here.'

She crouched down and examined the dents in the ground. They had faint ridges, and each one was about the size of a large box of matches. 'It can't be a table, or even a chair, but it might be a stool,' she said, holding her hands up so they pointed towards each other but didn't meet in the middle. 'Something where the legs are quite spread apart, but the top's quite small.'

It didn't make sense. Why would someone – presumably Bert – bring something like that out to the middle of the forest?

And where was G-Mamma while all this was going on? Just thinking about her mad SPI:KE gave Janey an idea. She looked directly into the blue eyeball they'd found. There was a white film across the pupil, and she wasn't at all sure that it could see her, but it was worth a try.

Sure enough, after just a few seconds her SPIV rattled on her chest, and G-Mamma's voice spurted out of it. 'Blonde! Where did you find that?'

'On the ground, near where the ptera dropped Trouble,' said Janey, holding up her SPIV necklace. G-Mamma's face loomed back at her, wearing a rather smug expression. 'Where are you?'

'I've got him, girly-girl!' G-Mamma's head dropped out of sight for a second, to be replaced by a pair of hypnotic green eyes. 'He's OK! Well, a bit chilly round the botty without his tail, but we're just sorting that out now.'

'But where are you? We want to see him,' said Janey.

And suddenly G-Mamma's eyes flitted furtively left and right. 'Well, you go home, Blondette, and you'll see little kitty really soon.'

'But I want to see—'

'NO!' screeched G-Mamma, so ferociously that Janey dropped the SPIV. Honestly, why was everyone shouting at her these days?

'All right,' she said crossly.

She popped the eyeball in her jeans pocket, then turned to James, who was poking around with a stick in the strange rectangular tracks. What were they? She should ask G-Mamma . . .

And suddenly it came to her. G-Mamma would never stop her from seeing Trouble.

It had to be a trap. Someone must have kidnapped G-Mamma, and possibly Trouble, and maybe even Bert, and they were trying to keep Blonde out of the way by luring her home.

'Nearest Spylab,' she said quickly to her Ultra-gogs. The enemy had probably taken G-Mamma and Trouble to a lab. They might be doing vile experiments on them even now. 'Quick!' she yelled.

The information that came up on the screen made her heart sink. Because the nearest Spylab did not belong to Solomon's Polificational Investigations. It was a black, hideous place, where Trouble had been tortured once before by evil overlord Copernicus.

It was Sunny Jim's Swims. And the instant he'd understood the location, James was off again.

17 black labs and bladders

Wishing she could have strapped her ASPIC on to her thigh over her jeans, Janey finally arrived at the Sunny Jim's Swims gates after Fleet-footing around the reservoir and across the footbridge which spanned the motorway. The pool complex was looking strangely derelict. There was certainly no sign of any customers, even though it was summer, and the kiosk blinds hung down at angles as if nobody had opened them in a long time. Not that that meant anything, thought Janey. There could still be a lab full of enemy spies downstairs.

Meanwhile, there was absolutely no sign of James. Her spy instincts kicked in again. James had taken off in too much of a hurry for it to be coincidence – almost as if he had his own mission. To . . . Janey hardly dared think it . . . to blow up the Spylab?

She quickly scanned the whole park, using her Ultra-gogs' X-ray vision to see though buildings and kiosks to the outlying areas. The only thing that appeared to be unusual was a bank of huge lights, strung up on scaffolding along one side of the picnic area. Janey ran across, searching for signs of enemies, or of James, but found only one thing – a pink feather.

'Jamie!' she called. 'Sable! G-Mamma . . .'

Luckily she'd been here before. Wading across to the middle of the toddler pool, she pressed the tiny S on the central sprinkler stand that she knew would lead her into the Spylab. The moment that she rolled out from under the entry tubes she realized that she had guessed correctly – or at least, partly correctly.

James was being thrown against the wall by some kind of gorilla. Janey's heart sank. Copernicus had been known to use gorilla henchmen to do his dirty work for him in the past; now one of them had hold of her brother and was dragging him forcibly across the glossy black floor of the Spylab. Towards what, Janey did not know.

'Stop!' she screamed. 'Take me instead. It's me – Jane Blonde.' And as the creature looked up at her from beneath its hairy, furrowed forehead, she ripped off her hat to show him her ponytail.

For a fraction of a second, she faltered. Surely gorillas didn't have blue eyes? And blue eyes that looked particularly pained and hurt to see her, even as its fur-covered hand closed around her brother's throat . . .

Wishing for her Girl-gauntlet, for *any* sort of

protection, she raced across the lab. James was cry-ing, great tears rolling down his cheeks as the creature strode backwards, dragging the boy by the collar. It was staring at her now, its strange blue eyes anguished, terrified . . . And now the hairy figure was opening its mouth and she accelerated, in case it was plan-ning on biting James, but instead a bitter roar was echoing around the lab . . . a cry of 'Owwwwwwww!' . . . or . . . wait, it sounded more like . . . 'Ouuuuuuut!'

She paused for a moment, surprised. But she didn't have time to wonder for long as the gorilla man thrust the body of her brother under the Spylab entry tubes. Again she stopped, confused by the action as James was immediately sucked up out of the Spylab to safety and the monster again screamed, 'Ouuuuuuut,' lunging towards her.

And it was then that she heard it.

Tick. Not the clock, because she could see that across the lab, the red figures telling her that it was 11.10. Ten past eleven.

Tick. There it was again, resonating around the black emptiness of the laboratory.

Tick. She should know that sound. Think, Blonde, she told herself, backing up against the bench as the gorilla reached out a hand . . .

Tick. She only remembered when she saw the wire trailing across the floor from what looked like a plastic bag of flour on the workbench. It was a bomb. A large watch was counting down the seconds. A watch she recognized. Her father's watch.

The gorilla was nearly upon her. She had about forty seconds to get out, if she had guessed correctly. The only exit was past the gorilla, and as she slid under the bench to escape its reaching, grabbing, leathery fingers Janey realized that she had just put even more distance between herself and the escape route.

She looked round in desperation. Above her was an odd circular skylight – obviously where one of the smaller pools had been at one time. The gorilla, its eyes glistening with . . . fury . . . or something Janey could not work out, was now running around the benches towards her.

Tick.

She had to go UP. That was the only way out. But there was not enough bounce in her Fleet-feet, and she'd used her SuSPInder and SPInamite. There wasn't even a chair nearby, just a small stepladder.

Tick. Muddy at the base. Tick.

A stepladder that Janey had seen before. That had been lying in a flower bed next to G-Mamma after the SPI:KE had miraculously appeared at her bedroom window on the night of Trouble's 'ceremony'.

Tick.

A stepladder that could well have been standing on boggy forest floor, causing four rectangular indentations in the mud.

Tick. Tick.

A stepladder that, now she thought about it, probably had special powers.

Tick. Tick. Tick.

The ticks were speeding up. There was nothing else for it.

Hoping desperately that she was right, Jane Blonde dragged the stepladder to below the skylight, tugged her hat back on, and then leaped on to the first rung, just as the ticks blended into one monotonous *beeeeeep* and she blasted up . . . up . . . and out of the Spylab.

18 blonde the bombshell

Head first, Janey rocketed through the skylight. Luckily her hat was no ordinary baseball cap; the PERSPIRE protected her skull and her face from the shattering glass, while the SPIsuit beneath her clothes repelled the towering tongues of flame that reached after her, burning her jeans straight off but leaving her body untouched. Janey went straight up in the air for several metres, then as the ladder began to drop back towards the ground she angled the far legs and hoped for the best.

Boing! The ladder hit the concrete next to the Sunny Jim's Swim's sign and took off again, bouncing Janey across the landscape as if she was on a giant pogo stick. All thoughts of what she had just left behind vacated her brain, and even though she could hear the rubble settling and moving behind her she wanted to laugh. This *had* to be another of G-Mamma's Wow and Weld creations. Her . . . Bladder?

Fun though it was, however, once again she didn't

know how to stop, and as she bounced across the motorway, to the stunned amazement of several truck drivers and a stream of cars, she realized that she didn't know how to turn it around either. And behind her, still cowering somewhere in the stark sunlight of Sunny Jim's Swims, was James. And G-Mamma, Trouble and Bert too, if, as she suspected, they'd been kidnapped.

As she thwacked into the ground again and the Bladder took off in yet another direction, Janey fumbled for her SPIV, yelling, 'G-Mamma . . .' as she bounced over a park bench looking out on to the reservoir. She couldn't keep hold of the SPIV and the stepladder; G-Mamma's face appeared at intervals in front of her as the visualator flew up and down as she leapfrogged the playground in the reservoir grounds, the boating lake, the ice-cream kiosk . . .

'Bouncing Blondes, what are you doing?' screeched G-Mamma.

'I'm on your stepladder thing,' said Janey. 'The Bladder. How do I stop it?'

'You're on the Blast-Off Ladder? How come?'

Janey screamed as she came very near to slicing her head off with a telephone wire. 'I found it at Sunny Jim's – were you there? – and now I need to get back to Jamie, but I can't . . . ow . . . turn it around or . . . ugh . . . stop it.'

'Jumping jimminies, I haven't worked out all the fine details yet.'

'Fine details? How to stop it?'

'It's something to do weight distribution, and I'm a teensy bit heavier than you. You'll never do it with your puny poundage!' G-Mamma's purple face loomed into view and then disappeared again. 'You'll have to jump, Blondette.'

The Bladder vaulted the park's boundary hedge, and Janey screamed again. 'We're heading for the high street. There are old ladies shopping . . . sorry, sorry,' she shouted to the pair of elderly women with shopping trolleys and a chihuahua on a lead whose heads she narrowly missed, '. . . and everyone can see me.'

'Get off that thing now, Blonde, and that's an order!' hollered G-Mamma.

Janey had no choice. The Bladder was about to bounce over a low-roofed church, where more old ladies were gathered in the courtyard, sipping tea. 'Map!' she said to her Ultra-gogs as two dozen sets of stunned eyes followed her pogo-ing progress over the toilet block. One more bounce and she'd be the main attraction in Winton town centre.

The flat church roof was just below her. Not at all sure what she was doing, Janey pushed the top of the stepladder forward, and to her joy the Bladder pointed down. As the front legs made contact with the rough surface of the roof and prepared to bounce off again, Janey threw herself backwards into a somersault and landed on both feet, feeling sick as the pain in her weakened ankle flared up again. Without any weight upon it, the Bladder fell forward, teetered over the edge of the roof, then slid down and planted itself upside down in a rose bush. That must be how G-Mamma had got off it too, Janey realized, remembering the SPI:KE languishing in the flower bed.

'I've stopped,' she said into her SPIV. Blue-haired ladies and the vicar were charging over to the upturned stepladder.

'Back to base,' barked G-Mamma. 'We were in the vicinity. Berty Bert's collected James – he'll be with you in four minutes.'

The crowd below was muttering threats about calling the police. The vicar called up to her, 'You are going to pay for this rose bush, I presume?'

Janey peeked over the edge of the roof. 'Oh, sorry about that. I'll . . . replace it for you.'

'I should think so.' One of the ladies elbowed her friend. 'Must be one of those circus kids. You never can trust them.'

'Circus kid – that's right,' said Janey. With a little bow, she jumped high enough to detonate her Fleet-feet, then somersaulted off the roof and down to the ground beside them. 'Solomon's Special Circus. On next week. Sorry about the roses. I'll just take this . . .' And grabbing the Bladder, she ran to the empty car park at the back of the church just as the Clean

Jean van pulled up. She opened the back doors, threw in the ladder and climbed in after it.

James turned to look at her from the front seat next to Bert as the van pulled away. Her brother was even paler than usual, the white of his skin contrasting starkly with his inky eyes.

'Are you OK?' Janey asked. 'You didn't get hurt by the explosion?'

James shook his head, but not before Janey spotted a large tear rolling down his cheek. He'd obviously been very shaken up.

'And what about you, Blonde?' said Bert gruffly. 'Nothing damaged?'

'No, I'm fine, thanks to G-Mamma's creation.' Janey wiped mud off the bottom of the ladder. 'Why were you there, Bert? I saw that you were at Sunny Jim's Swims too. I thought you'd all been kidnapped!'

Bert flushed a little and pulled his hat down over his eyes. 'We were sorting out Trouble, and . . . yeah, sorting out Trouble.'

'He's OK?'

'More than OK, JB. He's fine.' Bert started to whistle through his teeth, a sorrowful little tune that sounded oddly familiar. What weren't they telling her?

It was evidently the end of the conversation, and they rode the rest of the way home in silence. The atmosphere felt impossibly gloomy, and it only got worse when Janey entered the Spylab at home to find a bevy of SPIs gathered round on collapsible chairs. Alfie and his mother were there, as were Tish and Magenta, and Rook and Blackbird with parents Eagle and Peregrine. G-Mamma was near the fridge buttering slices of bread, and Janey's mum was loading them up with ham and tomatoes. There was a small mountain of sandwiches at the end of the bench; quite who was meant to eat them, Janey wasn't sure.

She went over to her mum. 'What's going on?'

Jean waved a piece of ham at her. 'Your father's organized a group briefing for two o'clock. He was quite insistent that everyone should be here.'

'Where is he then?' said Janey, looking around. Everyone *was* there, except for him.

'He'll turn up in a minute, I'm sure,' said Jean, although the smile she gave Janey seemed rather small and forced. 'Are you all right, sweetheart? I hear you had a bit of a scare.'

'That's right, Blonde the Bombshell,' cried G-Mamma, before Janey could so much as nod. 'Having to FLEET-FOOT your way out of that Spylab, and RUN all the way to Winton WITH JAMES. You must be exhausted.'

Janey held back a smile. G-Mamma didn't want anyone knowing about her strange Bladder invention, and she could quite understand why. 'We're OK.'

She wasn't actually convinced that James was all right. He'd positioned his chair near the window and was gazing soulfully through the gaps in the blinds, apart from the others. Thankfully Alfie had noticed too and was heading over to him with a soccer magazine under his arm.

By now it was 2.40 p.m., and people were starting to check their watches and shift uneasily in their chairs. Jean put the top on the last sandwich and sliced it in two. 'Hand the plates round, Janey. We might as well have these while we're waiting for your father.'

So they ate ham sandwiches and passed the next two hours giving each other updates on the summer holidays. By far the biggest excitement had been the rescue of James and the appearance of the prehistoric creatures.

'And this thing was really a velociraptor?' asked Tish sceptically. 'How do you know?'

'Well, I didn't exactly ask it,' said Alfie, bristling, 'but it looked just like that thing in *Jurassic Park*.'

Janey backed him up. 'And the pterodactyl too. That's chained up at the zoo now – Dad might let us see it if we ask him.'

Meanwhile Alfie had marched over to the computer and started bringing up information. 'That's what it looked like, isn't it, Blonde?' he said, pointing to the screen.

'It did.' Tish and Janey joined him at the computer.

'"The prehistoric creature of the Cretaceous period

is believed to belong to the family from which birds are descended"',' read Tish. 'Did it, like, fly?'

'No, it didn't, like, fly; it just, like, tried to kill us with its slasher claws and its big ugly teeth,' said Alfie crossly. 'But these other things flew – like those sparrows with teeth. And the pterodactyl.'

Tish leaned across him and typed something into the computer. 'OK . . . sparrows with teeth. That would be an . . . an ibero . . . iberomesornis from the Cretaceous period. And the pterodactyl is . . . hang on . . . a flying reptile from the Jurassic through to the Cretaceous period.' She shook her head. 'That cannot be real. Your dad is playing some trick on you,' she said to Janey.

'Or,' hissed Alfie, his eyes round, 'it *is* like *Jurassic Park*. He's turning Solfari Lands into some prehistoric zoo called, um, Cretaceous Creatures or something. Far out!'

But Janey shook her head. 'I'm pretty sure that G-Mamma had something to do with the sparrows,' she said under her breath as the SPI:KE's head whipped suspiciously in her direction. 'And it's not Dad. It's something to do with Copernicus. There was a gorilla at Sunny Jim's.'

Tish rolled her eyes. 'Right. So was it an ordinary gorilla, or one from the Cretaceous period?'

'I don't know,' was all Janey would say, getting irritated by Tish's lack of faith. 'I just know it was a gorilla-man, like the ones Copernicus made before. Or a man-gorilla. Or . . . or something like that.'

Now she thought about it, she wasn't really sure it was 100 per cent gorilla. It was hairy and humpbacked, for sure, but it had those strange eyes, and seemed to have some ability to speak. And . . . well, she couldn't really remember much beyond that. Before she could think any more about it, however, her mum clapped her hands at the front of the room.

'Erm, it's getting on for half past four,' she said, a little nervously. 'I don't know what's happened to Boz, but we can't keep you here for nothing. So . . . well, I know a bit about what he was going to brief you on, so I'll fill you in now, and then we can all just get on with it.'

'But he's the boss! Bozzy the Bossy. Shouldn't we wait another hour at least?' G-Mamma looked quite affronted, but Bert stood up slowly.

'Seems to me that the boss man would hardly choose to miss his own meeting. I reckon we should hear what his missus has to say.'

There were various murmurs around the room, and G-Mamma wriggled her shoulders and gave up. 'Go on then, Gina Bellarina.'

Janey's mum flicked a switch and projected a map on to the fridge. 'Well, here goes. But first, James, you've had a shock – I'd like you to go and have a lie-down.'

James shook his head violently and Janey's mum looked as if she was about to start getting firm with him, but Alfie gave him a little shove. 'Go on, mate. Take my soccer mag.'

His black eyes glittering with tears, James left the room. Jean waited a few moments and then cleared her throat. 'You may be aware that there have been explosions in Spylabs around and about.' She pointed to the locations of the Sol's Lols HQ, Solfari Lands, the Hallidays' house and Sunny Jim's Swims, then over to Florida. 'Someone is after something in the Spylabs.'

Janey put up her hand. 'Copernicus is still in his case at NASA,' she said, 'but I saw a gorilla like one of his henchmen over at Sunny Jim's . . . I think.' Actually the black Spylab now seemed like a dream, seen through a thick fog. 'Did you see it, G-Mamma?'

'At Sunny Jim's Swims? No, no,' said G-Mamma, sinking her teeth into a Dunking Dough Ball. 'I oggnt gere.'

'But I thought you went . . .' Just as Janey was about to argue, G-Mamma frantically crossed her eyes at her above the doughnut. Keep quiet, the message clearly said. 'Sorry,' said Janey. 'I made a mistake. I'm sure there was a gorilla there though.'

Again there was a rumble of discussion, and then her mother continued. 'The trouble is, Boz doesn't know what they're after, or whether it's already been taken in one of these raids that

151

have already happened. So there's really only one thing for it.' She looked down at her hands for a moment, as if she could hardly believe what she was going to have to say. 'We're going to have to destroy all the Spylabs to keep Boz's secrets safe.'

'All of them? The Copernicus black labs as well?' said Eagle, jumping off his seat.

'All of them.'

There was a stunned silence as the scale of the operation sank in. All the Spylabs. Throughout the world.

'Obviously we have to get rid of the labs with minimum damage,' explained Janey's mum. 'Boz has developed a special explosive based on SPInamite, which can be completely enclosed and not affect anything outside it. We are trying to get rid of equipment only,' she added seriously, 'not humans.'

Mrs Halliday stood up. 'When do we start?' she asked, ever practical. 'Only the children are back at school next week, and I'd like to make sure the old lab at Winton Primary is dealt with before then.'

Gina Bellarina looked around. 'We start tonight.'

And Janey watched the backs of the excited SPIs as they gathered around the globe that Gina placed on the table, choosing their targets. It was a terribly sad mission, destroying all her father's work. And why wasn't he there to tell them himself? This just wasn't making sense.

19 star of the spy film

Janey sat with Trouble on her knee as the calls came in from around the world. He shifted around uncomfortably and occasionally twitched the stump where his tail had been, as if it was still there. G-Mamma had whisked him off for repairs as soon as she had found him in his sorry state, but his golden plumage couldn't be restored.

Janey stroked his head. 'I'm sure it will come back when you're well enough to go through the Wower again,' she told him, and he rubbed his head against her hand. It was a much quieter kitty that had come home, and he only wanted to be around G-Mamma, Janey or Maddy. Or, of course, his beloved master, who had still not returned after two whole days.

Gina paced the lab, peering into her SPIV every few minutes and dropping it despondently each time. 'Do you think he's all right?' she asked for the hundredth time that day.

'Let me go and look for him.' But Janey already knew the answer – her mum hadn't wanted to let her out of her sight since the briefing session where Boz had failed to show.

'No, you stay here. I'd like you to help me tick off the Spylabs,' said Jean. 'You've been to so many of them, it would really help me if you could go through them with me.'

Janey sighed quietly, then tipped Trouble gently off her knee towards the door and went to her mum's aid. 'Florida, in the back of the villas,' she said. 'Eagle and Peregrine have done that one. The black lab at Cape Canaveral had already been dealt with. Then there's Antarctica, labs for SPI and for Copernicus – Alfie and Tish are there doing those right now.' She felt a twinge of annoyance. It should have been Al Halo and Blonde, the former ace team.

Her mother moved around the globe, putting stickers over the sites that had been SPInamited or SPIroscoped out of existence. 'The one on Copernicus's planet – G-Mamma and Bert are covering that,' she said. 'Where else? Aren't there any others?'

'Solfari Lands, Sol's Lols – all destroyed,' said Janey wearily. 'Mum, can't I just—'

'I want you here, Janey, out of harm's way!' Her mum grabbed the SPIV again and threw it back down in despair. 'And James. Where is he?'

'In his bedroom.' Ever since the black-lab experience, James had spent an awful lot of time lying on his bed, staring morosely out of the window. He wasn't allowed to walk to the zoo on his own any more, and he wasn't taking it well.

'Go and get him,' said her mum. 'I've got something you can both do close to home.'

Curious, Janey dragged James reluctantly up to the lab, where her mother was pulling something out of a drawer. 'This should be enough,' she said, handing Janey a bag of white powder, two wires – one red and one blue and a cheap digital watch from the petrol station.

'What is it?' Janey thought she had seen it before, but she couldn't remember where.

'Powdered SPInamite. The plastic bag it's in is actually an expanding membrane – Spy Film. It fills the room to the very corners, so the explosion is contained and nothing outside the room will be harmed, apart from a tiny bit of short-term memory loss if you're too close when it goes off. Isn't your dad clever?' Janey's mum smiled sadly.

'So,' said Janey, hardly daring to believe it, 'are we going to be allowed to take out a Spylab?'

'It's quite a special one,' replied her mother. 'You might want to take out some of the most personal belongings first.'

And she led them downstairs to the back door.

'G-Mamma's garage,' said Janey. 'Makes sense. But she's not going to be happy.'

'That's why we're doing it now. Here are the instructions – poke the wires through the Spy Film and out of the back of the watch, set the timer . . . and off you go. Give yourself plenty of time to get out.'

Janey nodded. 'Come on, Sable. Let's do it.'

As their mother disappeared back up the stairs, Janey and James ran to the garage. It seemed terribly sad to be blowing up the glamorous little lab that G-Mamma had created for herself, but in spite of that, Janey couldn't help feeling rather pleased. They were being trusted with something important, instead of being protected into a state of complete boredom.

James was already through the door, so Janey followed him with the SPInamite powder in its bag of Spy Film, trying to read the instructions at the same time. She found James leaning over the fat old tyre that was all that remained of the original garage, looking puzzled. 'What is it?' she asked.

She'd startled him. James jumped, then pointed at the tyre. Only then did Janey realize what was inside. 'Oh! Poor Trouble,' she said. The Spycat had the front of his body draped over the rubber of the tyre, while his back end dangled in the hole. 'It must make his bottom more comfortable. Let's take that outside.'

Between them they dragged the enormous tyre out on to the lawn, complete with cat. Then Janey took a few minutes to look round the lab, seeing which of G-Mamma's personal belongings she should save. There was far too much make-up to put aside, so Janey picked out G-Mamma's favourite Mermaid Magic eye-shadow and grabbed a packet of doughnut holes from the fridge. These she stashed outside the garage door, with G-Mamma's black wellington boots – the very boots G-Mamma had been wearing when Janey first met her outside the school gates.

Janey sighed. It felt like the end of something special, and when she saw her mum run out of G-Mamma's back door and into their own house, she knew that something else was afoot. She didn't have to wait long – just a few seconds later there was the same dull *bawump* sound that had accompanied the explosion at the Hallidays', and a vast cloud of glittery dust billowed out of the upstairs window of G-Mamma's old Spylab, next to Janey's room. It was gone.

It was all Janey could do not to cry, but James was looking at her with such terrible concern in his eyes that she pulled herself together. 'Blonde, you've got a job to do,' she told herself sternly. 'You ready, Sable?'

With one last longing look at the tyre, as if he would much prefer to join Trouble in there, James nodded and headed back through the garage door. Janey took a quick look around outside – nobody there – and followed him.

It really was a shame, she decided, that she

couldn't be in the room to see what happened when the SPInamite was detonated. It might have been rather fun to see the Spy Film expand to cover every wall, the floor, the ceiling, and then watch everything within it get obliterated. Like blowing something up inside a balloon, she thought.

'Blue wire, Jamie . . . I mean, Sable,' she said as she fed the red one through the Spy Film as the instructions directed. 'Then we take off the back of the watch – thank you – and put the wires in it like that.'

The parcel sat on the table between them like a small sack of flour. It looked so harmless. And yet so . . . familiar. Well, of course it was, she told herself. There was a diagram right there on the paper in her hand.

Janey set the watch to count down for thirty seconds and smiled reassuringly at James, who was already backing towards the door. 'It's OK. Go on, I'm coming too,' she said. She bent down to the bag to check that the watch was set, then ran outside.

The door banged shut behind her, and her head was suddenly filled with the image of a skylight. Or rather, of bursting through a skylight and of James being dragged under the entry tubes by the gorilla, getting sucked up the cylinder before the explosion, as if he had been . . . evacuated to safety? But that didn't make sense. The gorilla was a Copernicus henchman. Why would it have rescued Jamie?

She stopped in the middle of the lawn, covering her ears as her own watch counted down: Ten, nine, eight, seven . . .

Tick. That had been what the other flour bag thing had been doing. Tick. Her father's watch. Tick.

And just as the garage expanded briefly as if it was blowing out its cheeks and then settled back down again, Janey stumbled to her knees and howled, 'Nooooo!'

The gorilla's blue eyes. Her father's watch. The gorilla screaming, 'Ouuuuut.' 'Get out, Janey,' he would have said if he could. If he'd had the time.

Because it hadn't been a gorilla. It was her father. She'd delayed his escape from the bomb he'd been investigating, because he was making sure she and James were safe. Boz Brilliance Brown had exploded, along with the black Spylab. And she, Jane Blonde, had as good as killed him.

But the memories surged briefly and then receded, so only a kernel of understanding remained in her head. She'd have to pass it on. Whatever was left. She had to tell the SPIs.

zoo's news

For the best part of a week, they took it in turns to plough through the debris at Sunny Jim's all day and night, but their frantic search brought up nothing apart from a couple of thick black hairs.

'He must have escaped,' insisted Janey's mum, scrabbling through the rubble with her bare hands.

Janey fought back a sob. 'He can't have. You've seen what those enclosed bombs are like. He was stuck, right here, because I was too stupid to realize what was going on.'

Mrs Halliday called over from the area where the entry tubes had been. For the last half-hour she and Alfie had been combing the area for signs that Boz could have got out. 'Nothing here, I'm afraid. Janey, are you absolutely sure it was him?'

'It *could* have been one of those gorilla henchmen,' Alfie said hopefully.

But Janey shook her head, miserable to the core.

Now that she'd remembered the panicked expression in the blue eyes, she had no doubts. Why her father had turned into a gorilla, she didn't know, but she could see now that for the last few weeks he'd been getting steadily more hairy, more gruff and hunched over, and just more . . . ape-like. One of his strange experiments, she supposed.

She looked over at James, remembering that he had become a boy instead of a monkey through the R-Evolution process. He had been getting ever more distressed since Janey's short-term memory of the bomb blast had been restored, seeming to think that it was his fault that Boz had been stuck in the laboratory. 'No,' insisted Janey repeatedly. 'It was me. I was the one who suggesting going over there, the one who didn't recognize him. It's my fault.'

She had never felt so utterly bereft in all her life. 'There's nothing here,' she whispered. 'Nothing at all.'

Her mum stood up and dropped the hairs she had found into a plastic bag. 'Alfie, would you take these and check them out in the Spyl— . . . oh.'

Jean Brown sank to her knees, looking ready to cry, and G-Mamma, who had been foraging nearby, patted her clumsily on the shoulder.

'Don't you worry, Gina B.,' she said kindly, her own eyes swimming with tears. 'I still have a few tricks up my sleeve. I'll get these analysed somewhere.'

And suddenly Janey had had enough. 'Where? Where can you do that, G-Mamma? We've destroyed them all. All the labs. Even this one which had a person in it. He's dead! We can't do anything else. He's just dead.'

And with everyone staring at her, either in sympathy or in horror at what she'd said, she fled from the bomb scene with a sob, and didn't stop running until she'd made her way across to the massive building site where James had been held captive. She clambered up to the cage at the top of Jamie's crane. Alone. She could be alone there. Huddled in the corner, Janey curled up with her head on her knees and bawled. Everything had gone wrong. Being back together as a family hadn't worked – Jamie was miserable all the time, her father was missing-presumed-dead, and her mum was the most unhappy she had ever been in Janey's whole life. At least when Jean hadn't known that Boz was alive and that she had a spy identity, she'd been content with her cleaning business and their life together. Their little life. Just Janey and Jean.

There was a scuffling sound outside the cage. It was James, his head cocked on one side, hardly even breathless from swinging from the nearest crane on a long hook, not knowing whether to approach. Janey spread her arms out and he jumped in his strange, slightly loping fashion, straight to her side. He already knew what it felt like to be separated from family. He understood.

Janey took him by the shoulders. 'Jamie, tell me honestly,' she said, her voice cracking a little, 'do you like being human?'

The little boy looked at her anxiously, then slowly shook his head.

'Do you wish you were still a chimp, like Belle?'

With a slightly shifty expression as if he didn't want to be found out, James stared sorrowfully into her face and then nodded. But then he pointed to himself, to his heart, and then to Janey.

Her eyes filled up again. 'I know. I love you too. But we've messed everything up, haven't we? We should have just left things the way they were.' After a few moments of tearful hugging, the pair slid down the crane into the crater, Jamie scuttling with all the dexterity of the monkey he had been, while Janey kept her SuSPInder to hand, just in case. They bypassed the reservoir and made their way out beyond the school.

Suddenly Janey grabbed James's hand. 'Hey, we're going past Solfari Lands. Let's go and see Belle,' she said on impulse. The joy in James's face was enough to make her smile, even in such sad circumstances. 'On three, we'll Fleet-foot over the fence. It's late now – nobody will see us. Ready? One, two . . .'

On 'Three!' they both sailed up in the air, still holding hands, and vaulted the high wire fence

163

with ease. It was dusk, and the animals were getting restless, noisier. Only the elephants seemed unusually quiet. Janey could hear Belle's familiar chattering from her cage some way behind the Elephant Enclosure. She pointed in Belle's direction and smiled at James. He would want to see her on his own. With a grateful hug, he scampered away.

Janey turned around slowly in the twilight, listening to all the amplified animal sounds on her SPI-Pod. Lions roared and little monkeys gibbered, sounding so close that Janey whipped around to check it wasn't one of Copernicus's apes. But then she heard another sound – a harsh caw, like the call of an enormous crow. For a moment her heart raced, but then she heard something much more friendly. 'G'day, ya great ugly bird. Brought you some food, so don't you go biting my hand off.'

'Thanks, Berty-Bert,' she heard G-Mamma say.

'Not you, ya daft sheila. The ptera.'

Despite her misery, Janey grinned. SPI might be collapsing, her whole family falling apart, but G-Mamma would never change. Turning down her SPI-Pod, she ran to the Amphibian House and zapped down to what used to be the Spylab.

It had been transformed pretty quickly into a vast pterodactyl cage. The enormous dino-bird sat on a perch the size of a tree trunk across one end, while Bert tossed skinned rabbits through the bars. 'There you go, you big chuck.' From her position flat out on a bench, G-Mamma peered at Janey from under a couple of cucumber slices. 'Just trying to reduced the swelling,' she explained. 'I've cried so much my eyes are like golf balls.'

'So you think Dad's dead too?' said Janey, the lump in her throat suddenly growing again.

'Who knows, Blondette? He's surprised us before, and I don't doubt he'll surprise us again.' G-Mamma sighed. 'In the meantime though, your mother will take over SPI. I'll be out on my beautiful little ear.'

'Why?' said Janey.

'Because she hates me!'

'No, she doesn't.'

G-Mamma shuddered. 'Well, she's totally jealous then. I was your father's right-hand woman for a decade when she didn't even know he was alive. Now she's taken over all my duties. At least I still have my music.'

Janey covered up her smile. 'Oh, yes – your video. I bet you didn't have time to shoot it in the end.'

Bert chuckled. 'You haven't even shown Blonde?'

'My art is personal!' snapped G-Mamma.

'G-Mamma! Did you make a video? Oh, please!' said Janey. 'I need cheering up. Please show me.'

G-Mamma looked torn for a fraction of a second, but she was obviously dying to show someone. Quick as a flash, she pulled a personal DVD player out of her bag, dusted the sugar off it and projected the image on to the ptera-cage wall. There was a bit of jagged film and then suddenly, as the music started, the lights came up on a familiar scene.

'And . . . action!' whispered G-Mamma, reliving every second.

'That's Sunny Jim's Swims!' Janey gasped at the film as G-Mamma, glorious in shimmering silk, emerged from the toddler pool looking tragic and then swayed like a belly dancer over to the picnic area. 'That's why there were all those lights! And why you didn't admit you were there.'

'Shh!' G-Mamma pointed at the screen. 'The song's starting.'

And Janey watched, stunned, as G-Mamma wafted among the picnic tables, half singing, half rapping, jumping from one table to another like a gymnast, and street-dancing like a star. Only a SPI would know that she had Fleet-feet on, and that the Wower had created the hypnotic glow around her. . . .

> 'You were always on a pedest-al
> But you are only mort-al
> The boss of me no more
> Since you threw me out the door . . .'

The Screen-G-Mamma rapped on in a mournful fashion, gazing soulfully into the camera.

166

Janey gasped. 'Is this about . . . my dad?'

'No,' said G-Mamma with a disdainful snort, but Bert laughed, suggesting otherwise. Suddenly there were two G-Mammas, then three, then a whole army of hip-hopping G-Mammas.

Janey gasped again. 'You used the SPI-clone!'

'Nah – computer graphics,' said Bert with a grin.

'But you hate computers!'

Bert nodded. 'Young Halo gave me a hand.'

'Alfie?' So that was what he'd been up to all summer. No wonder he hadn't been pestering her for missions and things to do. 'Why wasn't I—'

'Quiet, it's the chorus,' shrieked G-Mamma, mimicking the glamorous rap star on the screen. She broke into song.

'I was all you were needing; now my heart, it's all
*   bleeding . . .*
Dripping on to the floor; I can't take any more.
And I am what I am, want to know where I stand;
So I'm telling you now, I'm taking things . . .'

The screen G-Mammas dropped their chins and glared into the camera . . .

'Into my own hands.'

As the song and the film clip finished, Janey

finally remembered to close her mouth. 'G-Mamma,' she whispered, 'you're . . . good.'

'I know!' The SPI:KE packed the DVD back into its case. 'Always told you I was, didn't I? And what's more, I've come up with some rather amazing discoveries recently, what with my Bladder, and the Cat's Eye Collar, and of course –' she reached over her shoulder to pull something out of a cylinder strapped to her back – 'my wonderful SParrows.'

Janey stared at the narrow pointed strip of wood in G-Mamma's hand. 'That's not a SParrow.'

'Well, I think I know what I invented, Blondette,' said G-Mamma with a toss of her head. Her green leggings and hooded tunic shimmered from her head to her feet and she was wearing a great cowl hood, and green pointed slippers on her feet. 'These are SParrows – SPI arrows, like I said – and here is my bow, and I . . .' and she gave a little twirl, '. . . am the new super-SPI, Robin Hoodie.'

Janey shook her head again. 'But that's not right.'

'It so is,' said G-Mamma with her hand on her hip. 'I'm Robin Hoodie, good good goody, save the poor from all things cruddy. See?'

'No, I mean those aren't SParrows, are they? I thought the SParrows were the toothy birds that were chasing you and Trouble past Seacrest and Argents. If you didn't create them, who did?'

'I don't know. They're something to do with

Trouble, I think. They only appeared after he started bringing half-dead birds into my Spylab. In fact, he's been having a very birdy time recently, what with chasing that turkey into Solfari Lands . . .'

As Janey listened to her SPI:KE witter on, a few things began to fall into place. 'These prehistoric birds that have been hanging around – maybe they're not from the past. Maybe they've been *created* from normal birds.'

'Hang on,' said Bert, staring at the SPI:KE. 'Now you mention it, Blonde, this ptera here is a bit like a hulking big cassowary without feathers. That's an Aussie bird, prehistoric-looking,' he explained to Janey.

'What was it Tish said about those vampire birds?' Janey whipped the PERSPIRE off her head and typed in what she could remember the red-headed Spylet saying. 'Iber . . . Ibero . . . there! Iberomesornis.'

And the world around her tilted on its axis. She checked 'velociraptor' again. 'Predecessor of modern birds', she read. Maybe . . . Maybe big birds, like turkeys. Janey grabbed hold of the pterodactyl-cage bars to hold herself upright. 'I've got it! It's Dad! He must have invented a new process. Like Rapid Evolution – the thing that evolved Jamie from a monkey to a boy – only . . .' she gulped, 'only this is the opposite. It DE-volves creatures, into what they would have been in the past.'

And now she knew for definite – it wasn't a gorilla she had seen. The eyes had been too intelligent; the creature still had a small capacity to speak. Not R-Evolution. Devolution.

'He was a caveman,' she said, shaking her head. 'Dad tried it on himself. He devolved himself into a . . . what do you call it – a prehistoric person?'

'Neanderthal,' said Bert.

It was all too much to take in. Janey slumped to the floor, staring at the ptera. It gazed back at her balefully, then nudged Bert through the bars for another rabbit. 'It's too weird. All this happening in our Spylabs.' The very same Spylabs that her father had wanted destroyed. It wasn't because there was an *enemy* after them. It was because this process was too dangerous. He wanted it to disappear.

Rather like he had himself. But why would he want to destroy his own labs? And why would James want them obliterated too? Was he to blame? As the thought ran through her head, Janey's jaw dropped.

'What?' cried G-Mamma. 'Talk to me, Blonde.'

'There's . . . There's another Spylab,' gasped Janey. 'It's still opening hours, so you haven't destroyed it yet.'

She leaped to her feet. 'Jamie!' she yelled into her SPIV. 'Sable, leave Belle. Meet me at the gate!'

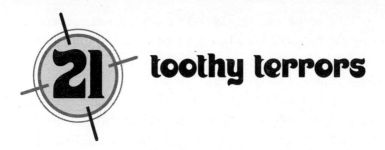

As they raced through the dark streets of Winton, Janey SPIVed Alfie. 'Seacrest and Argents,' she panted.

'Now?' Alfie's outraged face bumped around in front of her. 'I am not buying uniform at eight o'clock at night. The footy's on in ten minutes.'

'Not uniform – Spylab!' Janey seized James's hand and steered him around a tight corner on to the high street.

There was a stunned silence and then, 'Be there in five. Shall I bring Mum?'

'And mine,' said Janey. There were a few good-byes to be said, and what was left of her family needed to be there.

Janey grabbed James's hand to speed him up. 'It's you, isn't it? The someone who's after something in the Spylabs.'

James took in a deep breath, then nodded, duck-ing away from Janey, fearful that she'd be angry.

'I knew I recognized those feet – in what I thought was my "dream", and in the video from Sol's Lols security. You've been going to Spylabs to find a machine. And Dad's been trying to stop you.'

They reached the glass doors to the department store, so Janey skidded to a halt and pulled her brother around in front of her. 'Just tell me if it's true,' she said gently, panting.

James paused, and then nodded again.

Janey threw her arms around him. 'It's OK. Everything will be OK.'

They turned to face the Seacrest and Argents doors and pushed. Nothing. Janey had only been there once before as a SPI, and G-Mamma had handled it all. She'd had some kind of swipe card to get through the doors. Janey didn't have one, so she ran around the side of the building to the window near the shoes.

'Biff it,' she said to James. He stared with surprise at his Boy-battler, then covered his eyes and smashed straight through the window.

'Good boy.' He was a good boy. And a great brother. Janey smiled at him as they bounced through the hole in the glass, then crouched down below the rails of Work Skirts for Women. 'Now I don't know where the lab is,' she said, 'but I'm guessing it's in the basement.

Hard as they looked, however, there was no sign of an entry tube like the ones they'd used in the other labs. Janey became more and more frustrated, shoving rails of clothes out of the way, pulling food off the shelves, even checking under the tills that all lay open like mouths with the tongue sticking out. 'It's just a shop,' she said bitterly.

James shrugged. He couldn't find anything either.

'But I'm sure it's here.' She sighed. 'Let's try the lift.'

Checking her watch, she pressed the button to call the lift up from the basement. Alfie should be here any moment, and so would her mum. 'Hurry up,' she said to the lift doors, willing them to open more quickly. They were enormous concertina doors like those in a warehouse. Not a very subtle way to get in and out of a Spylab. What if she was wrong?

But then the doors finally opened, and Janey discovered that her spy instincts had been absolutely spot on. 'Aah – mind out!' She pushed Jamie behind her and tried to work out what to do as three tiny, vicious birds shot through the doors, followed by eleven or twelve more as the concertinas folded back, revealing not one, but three velociraptors and what appeared to be . . . 'a mammoth?' whispered Janey.

James had frozen behind her. The prehistoric sparrows were buzzing and snapping at their heads like a swarm of enormous mosquitoes, and as Janey tried to fend them off, one of them tore through the skin on the back of her un-Gauntleted left hand, and she cried

173

out. The velociraptors, each of which had been taking its time to leave the relative safety of the lift, turned their fanged heads towards the Spylets and bobbed through the doors. They were only metres away. The mammoth blundered past them, head down, clothes and sensible shoes scattering around it, various coloured blouses speared on its enormous tusks.

'Argh!' Another iberomesornis had attacked, and one of its partners made for James, aiming straight for his eyes. Janey flicked open her titanium blade and jabbed upwards. 'See how you like it!' she yelled.

Mistake. Now the velociraptors had them well within their sights. James seemed completely incapable of moving, and for a second Janey was reminded how he was never intended for a spy life. Or even for a human life. Though quite who would be OK with fighting off velociraptors in their local department store, she couldn't really say.

The nearest one was baring its vicious teeth just centimetres from her nose. Janey grabbed Jamie's right hand, dragged it through the crook of her arm and used it to smack the creature under the chin with his Boy-battler. The brick-weight glove sent the monster soaring across menswear; hangers and shelves crashed to the floor, trapping the first velociraptor underneath, its slashing claws flailing helplessly.

'One down,' said Janey. 'Oh no.'

As she turned to speak to James she noticed the

mammoth rolling its head from side to side in a rather threatening fashion. Its mean little eyes were fixed on her ponytail – it looked as though it intended to spear it with its tusk. Janey didn't know a lot about mammoths (although she did suddenly understand why the elephants at the zoo had been so quiet – they weren't actually there any more). She was fairly sure, however, that getting caught beneath a running mammoth would not be pleasant. She spun round. The other two velociraptors had tired of nosing through the frozen chickens and were heading back in their direction. Mammoth behind, velociraptors in front – it wasn't much of a choice.

'Up!' yelled Janey as the mammoth trumpeted deafeningly and then charged. James Fleet-footed on to her shoulders. The nearest velociraptor had hold of her Girl-gauntlet. Squeezing her finger, she injected a heat-seeking missile straight down the creature's gullet, then she took a firm hold of Jamie's knees and bounced on to the balls of her toes. *Thwump!* Her Fleet-feet detonated and the two of them shot upwards like a human totem pole, Jamie's head brushing the sprinklers on the ceiling. The mammoth shot beneath Janey's feet, careening into one exploding velociraptor and almost flattening another.

The remaining velociraptor was now extremely fed up. Limping badly on a crushed leg, it stumbled across the store floor towards them, screeching

venomously. The mammoth had slid into piles of shopping baskets and was shaking them off as it started on
the return path towards the Spylets, and half a dozen
of the needle-toothed sparrows were also tearing
towards them.

They were surrounded, being pushed into the
centre of the store, where the quadrangle of tills sat
under a 'Please pay here' sign. Janey pulled James over
the nearest desk and they cowered together on the
floor. Close, far too close, they could hear the baying
of the velociraptor and the steady thud of the paws of
whatever was coming up the stairs. They were going to
be torn apart by a bunch of prehistoric monsters, in a
downtown Seacrest and Argents. Nobody would ever
believe it – even if the creatures left anything for them
to find.

But this . . . this wasn't just any Seacrest and
Argents! 'Oh!' She couldn't believe it. Janey had been
behaving as if the store was an ordinary shop, when all
the time she knew it was a spy store. She leaped up on
to the top of a till, spotted a sprinkler and shouted as
loudly as she could, 'Wow me!'

The next second the whole floor was cloaked in a
fine, damp mist, sparkling against the dark sky outside.
Through the glitter Janey saw Alfie and his mother
peer through the window followed immediately by the
sound of shattering glass. The two Halos and Gina
Bellarina tumbled into the store, dropping into combat

positions. 'You don't scare me,' growled Mrs Halliday to the velociraptor. 'I've got nasty teeth too.'

Most of the creatures had turned their attention towards the trio who had just entered. Alfie was already shouting 'Bring it on, you big Dumbo,' to the mammoth, preparing his Boy-battler for a mighty great thump, and Janey's mum had leaped on to its back, wrapped her SuSPInder around its tusks and was attempting to steer it into the ladies' changing cubicles.

But Janey had forgotten that she and James were already in their spy gear when they entered the store. Going through the store-wide Wower had transformed them from their spy gear into their everyday outfits of jeans and a T-shirt. There was nothing to protect them from the vicious onslaught of the squadron of killer sparrows, and Jamie cried out as two attacked him from either side. Janey tried jumping down to help him but a beak caught at her elbow and she screamed, pain searing through her arm. They were going to be ripped to shreds, but if she Wowed again then the others would find themselves in their ordinary clothes, unprotected, vulnerable . . .

Suddenly there was a thunderous roar above their heads. Janey looked up through the skylights to see the undercarriage of a familiar plane, except that now it had been Wowed and Welded. It had two enormous wheels – Janey could see that one was her

177

old inflatable paddling pool, and the other was now painted white with daisies on it. Last time she'd seen it, that tyre had been in G-Mamma's garden, cushioning Trouble's bottom. The Pet Jet touched down lightly on to the solid store roof, and out jumped G-Mamma and Bert. They crashed through the skylight, a loud cawing sounding from above their heads.

'Ptera!' She cringed and dropped down automatically, but to her amazement the beast swept by her and jabbed at the velociraptor, which was rather getting the upper hand of Agent Halo.

'Get off my mum, Pterodactyl!' screamed Alfie, leaping straight over the tills, but then a voice called out, 'No worries, mate, she's on our side now. Aren't you, PTerror?' Bert raced around the outskirts of the store, shouting directions and lobbing bits of meat into the air.

The monstrous little sparrows were still intent on dissecting Janey and James, however, and Janey turned back to swat at one that was about to take a chunk out of the boy's ear, only to find that it turned on her and clamped its teeth around her finger instead. She screamed, the pain unbearable . . .

'Robin Hoodie brings the goodies!' The cry came from somewhere over Janey's head. She looked up, batting away another bird, blood dripping from both arms, to find G-Mamma in her green outfit, bow in hand, shooting from the top of the Bladder on which she was bouncing around the store. Trouble, Wowed but minus his tail, was lashed to a lower step of the Bladder, having huge fun lashing out with his sabre claw, exacting his own sweet revenge on the evil sparrows. Maddy and PTerror circled above, driving the birds back into the centre of the room to be dispatched by the SWAT team of Robin Hoodie and her merry cat.

Janey jumped down beside Jamie. He was nursing his head, and blood flowed from a gash behind his ear. 'The Wower will sort that out,' said Janey, giving him a hug.

But then she remembered that the boy needed more than a Wower to help him. 'Let's go,' she said, and she pushed him down the first entry tube behind the tills and jumped down the second herself.

It was time.

 **devolving dads**

The dimly lit Spylab was the biggest Janey had ever seen, stretching the whole length of the Seacrest and Argents building. Advanced spy equipment lay the full length of the centre of the room, lined up like exercise bikes at an upmarket gym – a DeSpies-U mirror and chair, a Crystal Clarification unit, a Wower that looked big enough to take a whole football team (or an elephant), and some items that Janey didn't recognize. The whole of the end wall was covered in shelves groaning with SPI-buys of every nature, ready to restock the Secret Agent displays upstairs.

'First things first,' said Janey, and she pushed James gently into the Wower cubicle, swapping places with him as soon as he emerged dressed once more as Spylet Jimmy Sable. 'Don't move,' she told him.

The Wower did a good job of soothing Janey's jagged nerves as it fitted her in fine Lycra and gadgetry, and she walked back out into the S&A Spylab feeling much more perky. Much more Blonde, in fact.

'Now, what we have to find is . . . Jamie? I mean, Sable?'

Janey tutted. That boy was impossible to pin down. Every time she asked him to stay somewhere he ran off. But that just made it all the more clear to her that she was in the right place at the right time. The room was completely silent. Janey turned up her SPI-Pod. There. She could hear him breathing. On tiptoe, not wanting to disturb any stray prehistoric creatures that might still be close by, she made her way down the lab.

'Jamie,' she whispered, 'don't worry. Everything will be all right. Just come out, wherever you are.'

His breathing, amplified in her SPI-pod, grew more rapid. He was starting to panic. Spylabs reminded him only of bad things – of being R-Evolutionized and separated from his sister, or fleeing from a building just as it was exploding. 'It's OK,' she crooned soothingly, like she did to Trouble when his fur was on end. 'I'm here now. It's OK.'

Reaching the loaded shelves, Janey pulled down a Back-boat and a pile of ASPICs as the breathing in her ear became ever more laboured. He was somewhere nearby, she knew it. Then she saw a flash of white to one side. The stripes on his

SPIsuit. Somehow he'd snuggled down in the corner between two sets of shelves, and only his hairy foot was sticking out. *Hairy?*

Jamie wasn't alone. Wrapped around his waist was a great pair of hair-covered arms. and over his shoulder loomed a hairy face with a broad nose, a bulging forehead and two bright blue eyes. Eyes that flashed with puzzlement and concern.

'Dad,' whispered Janey. She dropped to her knees and put out her hand. 'You're here. You're alive!'

But to her shock, her father shook off her hand and tightened his grip around Jamie, shaking his head and grunting. Drawing up his knees, he gathered Jamie into his lap and sheltered him from Janey.

'I'm not going to hurt him,' said Janey, although she was rather hurt herself. Her own father was barely recognizable – but surely he was still capable of normal human emotions, like being pleased to see his daughter?

And again the Neanderthal version of her father threw his great head from side to side, guttural gnashing sounds coming from his mouth.

'Dad, you . . .' Janey paused, her heart sinking. She had to check. 'You are my dad, aren't you?'

The blue eyes studied her, puzzled, then sharpened for a moment. With a furry finger he drew in the dust on the back of a nearby shelf. B. O. Z.

'Prove it,' said Janey.

Again that puzzled slant of the head, then a brief blast of brilliant blue as he held up his hand, now almost completely covered with hair, but with half a thumb missing, where the original Clarification had damaged him. Janey felt a sob catch in the back of her throat. It *was* him, even if there was very little left of the old Boz, her lovely father and wonderful SPI leader.

'I can't believe you're alive. So you . . . you must have Satispied out of Sunny Jim's to Solfari Lands,' said Janey softly.

Boz scratched his face for a few moments, then held out his palm and clumsily pressed the middle of it with a thick finger. The Satispy remote control. And then he'd hitched himself a ride on an elephant, too weak to go under his own steam or dare to Satispy again, but knowing there was one last place he had to get to.

'So all this – all the Spylabs being blown up – that was you. Your orders. Because you didn't like what you'd created.' She didn't need to wait for the nod that followed the long pause to know that she'd hit on the truth. 'You . . . That night you told me I'd had a dream, you got caught out! Jamie . . . Jamie was trying to use your devolution machine . . . and you stopped him, and you fell. You devolved by accident!'

Nodding slowly, Boz tightened his grip on Jamie and the boy cried out, whether in fear or in pain Janey wasn't sure. 'Dad,' she said gently, waiting anxiously for the blue eyes to clear again, to reveal some element of the human still inside him. Then more loudly, 'DAD!' The eyes focused, although the Neanderthal head was still rolling on the thick neck.

'You have to let him go,' she said, holding her arms out for Jamie. 'Let go . . . please.'

But just as it looked as though Boz was about to release his grip on James, there was a scuffling sound from under the entry tubes, and G-Mamma's voice echoed down the room. 'Blonde, are you in here?'

'Here!' shouted Janey.

'You have to get out. I can hear the bomb. It's rigged to blow, but I can't see the timer.'

Suddenly a hairy hand tapped Janey's arm and her father held up ten fingers.

'Ten o'clock,' she shouted to G-Mamma. 'It will go off at ten. What time is it now?'

'Nine twenty-eight,' yelled G-Mamma, scooting towards them on Rollerblades, bow and SParrow at the ready. 'Are there more of those beasties down there?'

'No, it's . . .'

But her father had hold of her hand again, and he released his grip on James enough for the boy to slip through his ape knees and collide into Janey. She tumbled backwards, her father's sharp fingernails raking her skin. 'What?'

Boz got to his feet, gibbering feverishly and holding up his hands again. Something – fear? – had sharpened his senses again, and he was trying to tell her something.

'The bomb? I know! It will go off at ten.'

'Ngggg,' bellowed her father, brandishing his hands in her face. 'Ngggggg!'

'No?' said Janey.

'What the hairy horrors is that?' bleated G-Mamma, drawing back her bow.

'Don't shoot – it's Dad.' Janey whisked around, catching hold of James's hand as he tried to scuttle past her. As G-Mamma stared aghast at the hunched figure before them Janey's stomach cramped. 'He was saying no. No. Not ten.' She held up her own hands and then bent one finger over. 'He hasn't got ten fingers. Nine and a half. Is that right?'

And the caveman creature that had once been her father looked from his daughter to his son, nodding as if desperate to communicate something. James pulled himself free and ran towards the line of equipment down the middle of the room, and the caveman stumbled after him.

Janey struggled up from the floor. 'Nine thirty! It's going to blow at nine thirty.'

'But that's in fifteen . . . ohhh,' said G-Mamma.

'Jamie, now!' screamed Janey, and the boy pelted with all possible speed towards a strange white doughnut the size of a playground roundabout. The R-Evolver! It started to spin as soon as his hand touched it.

James jumped on to the springy disk, positioning himself to sit on the edge. Hollering, Boz stretched out to pull him off the device, flinging James aside as the R-Evolver spun more quickly anticlockwise, mysterious dark and light pulsing in the centre like stage smoke. Boz missed his footing; instead of jumping clear as he meant to, the thick-set caveman body of Janey's father slipped, lunging, tipping forward. 'Dad,' screamed Janey, 'stop!' But he overturned completely, and the cylinder of horrible nothingness in the middle of the spinning machine split as if slashed with a knife, swallowing him whole, encasing him in the darkness.

'He's disappeared . . .' screamed Janey, just as G-Mamma shot to her side.

'Four seconds, Blonde,' cried the SPI:KE, as she enveloped both Spylets in her vast green embrace and the shimmering force field of her USSR – her Undetectable Spy-Shield Raiser spy ring – boomed around them.

There was a searing flash of light, whiter than the purest white that Janey had ever seen. Crying out and covering their eyes, the spies huddled together. The Spylab flew apart into a billion microscopic particles, and with it went the immediate memories of Jane Blonde, G-Mamma and Spylet Jimmy Sable.

# tyre tracks

They emerged, unharmed apart from their short-term memory loss, into a scene of devastation. Slain vampire-like birds and velociraptors were littered across counters and clothes racks, and the other SPIs were wiping themselves down with towels pilfered from the Housewares department.

Gina Bellarina was the first across the floor as they reached the top stair. 'Jane Blonde, will you stop getting yourself blown up? What is wrong with this family?'

'Yeah, you have all the fun,' said Alfie morosely, although he was nursing his slashed right arm rather proudly. 'And where did that come from?' He pointed greedily at the jet.

'You were down there a long time,' said Mrs Halliday. 'Anything interesting?'

Janey, James and G-Mamma all gaped at each other. 'There was . . . There was something,' said

Janey. 'Someone else there . . . or . . . No, that must just have been when you turned up, G-Mamma.'

'Funny you should say that, little spy people,' said G-Mamma, dusting down her enormous knuckle-duster of a spy ring. 'I can't help feeling there was something down there. I had my SParrow ready to fend off . . . something – nearly shot myself in the foot when we crouched under the force field.'

Jamie, of course, could say nothing, but he kept patting down his body and scratching at his arm, then sighing as if he was hugely disappointed. Janey wrapped an arm around him, picking a sweet wrapper from his shoulder – a tiny square of film. Of . . . spy film. Hadn't she once had some on her head, just like that? Anyway. James. Something was bothering him – maybe he would tell her later. When they were alone. When everything was back to normal.

But nothing felt right for the whole of the rest of the week. There were things that were significantly *wrong*, for sure. Her father was still missing. Gina refused to believe he might be dead, so at the SPI-wide debrief they all vowed to carry on as if he could walk in the room at any time. They would uphold all SPI principles at all times and, for now, Gina Bellarina would stand in as head of SPI. 'Who'd have thought it?' said Gina with a giggle. 'Mops and buckets one minute, spies the next.'

G-Mamma straightened her shoulders. 'If it's too much, Gina B., I'd be happy to . . .'

The Hallidays exchanged glances with Janey, but laughed along with everyone else when Bert said, 'Come on, G-Mamma. You've never done any cleaning in your life.'

'I didn't mean the Clean Jean duties, Agent Dubbo Seven,' said G-Mamma frostily. 'I meant SPI.'

With new-found diplomacy Gina said, 'G-Mamma, I'll be glad of your help wherever you can provide it. I'm sure we'll manage if . . . if we all pull together.'

Meanwhile the start of the new school year drew ever closer, and they still hadn't got all their uniform. Unable to face a visit to Seacrest and Argents, Janey persuaded her mum to take them to the next town, and they wandered listlessly around the shops, picking up bits and pieces. Janey missed her dad. She missed her mum too, when it came to it, now that she was so busy. But poor James seemed even more distraught than ever.

'Drop us off at Solfari Lands, Mum,' suggested Janey. 'We'll go and see Bert and the PTerror, and check in on Belle. You'd like that, wouldn't you, Jamie?'

A tear rolled down his cheek as he nodded, gripping her hand fiercely.

'Oh, that's a good idea, Janey,' said her mother.

'I've got meetings with two heads of state this evening. That'll give me some time to get ready.'

Heads of state, pondered Janey later as she watched James and Belle communicating excitedly through sign language. It was much too hard for her to understand. But then, so were things like 'meetings with heads of state'. She didn't even know what that meant. And, just for a moment, she longed for the time when her mum's main job had been just that – being Janey's mum. Eventually, tearing James away from Belle, Janey SPIVed Alfie.

'Last day before school,' she said.

'Tell me about it. Those sleeves haven't got any shorter,' said her friend. 'I'm going to look like an idiot.'

Janey laughed, then said, 'Hey, Jamie's really sad. Will you come and play footy with him?'

'Let me think.' In the little screen on her SPIV, Alfie put a finger on his chin. 'Hmm, help Mum label my school underpants? Or play footy? Pants. Footy. Footy. Pants . . . I dunno. It's a tough one.'

'See you in a bit,' said Janey with a grin.

At least Alfie was the same as ever. She was so glad her best friend was going to the same school as her. It would be awful to have to start all over again. She looked at James, trailing behind her at a snail's pace as he walked backwards, staring at the zoo. He'd had to start all over, poor thing. Completely all over.

A new species. That was why she'd taken him to the Spylab.

Janey stopped short. That was it. She remembered now. That was why she'd dragged James off to the Spylab – to find the devolution machine. But now the last Spylab was gone. The last of her father's creations. All gone. There was nothing she could do.

Janey sighed as she vaulted the back fence into the garden. The football was lying next to the garage. Even that was just an ordinary garage now. G-Mamma was living back in her old room, rebuilding the Spylab piece by piece with her vast array of rather peculiar home-made equipment, which included a Wowed-and-Welded ceiling fan that flew around slicing the heads off things, and a Trouble-sized Segway made from a broken music stand, on which he zipped around with glee, his tail stump swishing furiously.

In fact, the only sign of what had happened was the artfully shrouded Pet Jet in the allotment. Even the turkeys had gone – the owner had accused G-Mamma of letting them escape or possibly eating them, and the remaining few had been relocated. Janey hopped over the allotment fence and peeped under the camouflage netting. That had been quite an adventure, flying a fighter jet. But now it was back to school, and there was no Boz, and the adventures would probably stop. In any case, thought Janey with a grin, the Pet Jet hardly looked like a sinister fighting machine, with one paddling-pool wheel and the other a great white tyre from the old Spylab. Janey dusted it off. There was glass on it. Tiny chips of glass and a splinter of wood. Wood from a . . . a window frame?

Janey stared, then touched the white ring as she peered back at the window to the Spylab. Sure enough, there was a tyre track straight down the middle of it. Her dream-that-wasn't-a-dream. Something had bounced off across the room and out of the window; had ended up in G-Mamma's garage; had fascinated Jamie – and not because of the birds that sat inside it . . . until they turned into prehistoric birds.

And as she turned back to the wheel of the Pet Jet a host of random images popped up in Janey's mind. A white doughnut, spinning. A . . . a caveman, stepping and slipping and falling into a hole. Her dad's eyes. Jamie. A cylinder of light that was black.

'R-Evolver!' gasped Janey. The old tyre was a R-Evolution machine – the very R-Evolver that had spun her father's genes backwards until he became a caveman. The strange whirl from her dream! *That* was the 'revolver' he'd shouted about. And if it could R-Evolutionize, it could also . . .

'Jamie,' she squeaked as her little brother approached, scanning the garden for his football, 'do you really, really, *really* hate being a human?'

James stopped dead, his eyes on the tyre. 'You know, don't you? You know what it is?'

James nodded slowly, and Janey understood what a world of information was in that nod. He wanted to turn back. With his finger, the boy made circles in the air. Clockwise for evolution. Anticlockwise for devolution. James gazed at her, his eyes flooded with tears.

And at that moment Janey made up her mind. It wasn't what her dad had wanted, it seemed, and she could see why. Her heart might break a little. Even a lot. But Jamie's completely shattered life could be mended.

'What's going on?' said a voice from the alleyway. Alfie skidded to a halt on his SPI-cycle and twitched the camouflage net to one side. 'Awesome. You're not going to fly that thing, are you?'

Janey shook her head. 'No. You are.'

Alfie's mouth fell open in delight. 'AWESOME!'

'Can you do it? You need to get it just above the ground and then hover.'

'Can I do it? I've done it millions of times . . . on the computer,' he added under his breath as he threw back the net and clambered up to the cockpit. 'I want to fly it properly though. Why hover?'

And Janey and James exchanged glances, doing the same little circular movement with their fingers. 'Because we need the wheel to spin. Don't land again until I tell you.'

'Whatever,' said Alfie, too beside himself with joy at the prospect of handling a fighter jet to care even remotely. 'Cover your ears!'

Janey and her brother stood back with their fingers in their ears as the Pet Jet sparked into life. The Wow and Weld had quietened the engines considerably, but it still sounded like four massive motorcycles starting up at once. There was a bit of a lunge to one side, then Alfie's hand moved behind the perspex, and the Pet Jet lifted jerkily into the air, the R-Evolver tyre hanging two metres above their heads.

Janey dropped to her knees beside James and gave him the biggest squeeze imaginable. 'I will miss you,' she told him, 'forever.'

Jamie signed, 'Me too.'

Dragging out the moments for as long as she could, Janey stepped slowly up to the plane's wheel. 'Up,' she said, and Jamie vaulted on to her shoulders without hesitation. Suddenly the weight disappeared from her shoulders; she put her head back to see James hanging on to the R-Evolver . . .

Alfie's SPI-cycle was propped against the fence – now Janey climbed up it, until she was balancing one foot on the saddle and another on the fence itself. If she stretched with her whole body, she could just reach the tyre. She went to turn it, but James shook his head. 'Oh right – that way's Rapid Evolution. We want Devolution. Bye . . . Jamie.' Reaching with the tips

195

of her fingers, Janey whizzed the wheel the way James needed her to.

She didn't know how she could bear to watch Jamie leave, clinging on to the R-Evolver as it spun ever faster. His features rapidly became a blur. Through parted fingers Janey could just see a melding of colour and shapes, and then the lines spun so fast before her eyes that she felt sick and turned away, jumping down from the fence, her heart pounding more loudly than the Pet Jet's thundering . . .

Not until she felt a tug at her leg did she look up.

A medium-sized chimpanzee swayed at her side in the buffeting jet stream. Janey looked down into the chocolate button eyes of her brother. Not her brother any more, she corrected herself. Belle's brother. The way it should be.

'Oh, Jamie,' she whispered. But he linked his finger and thumb together to give her the 'OK' sign. And somehow she knew that it would be.

Behind her a window was flung open. 'Who the heck's flying my Pet Jet?'

'Oops!' Janey hastily signalled for Alfie to land. He took no notice, but grinned and waved as he soared up to 1,000 feet and then – BOOM! – he took off across the skies.

'It's Alfie, sorry. Oh, G-Mamma,' said Janey, smiling as she took hold of James's hand, 'Jamie seems to have turned himself back into a chimp. Do you think

Bert could take him to Solfari Lands? I think he'd like to see Belle.'

G-Mamma rolled her eyes. 'Now, however did that happen, Janey Brainy?' But she looked as if she had a pretty good idea.

24 everdene, ever blonde

'Maths four times in one week,' moaned Alfie, stuffing his timetable into his pocket. 'That is just sick.'

The timetable at Everdene was different, it was true. Moving around the school to different teachers was a bit of a shock to the system too, but Janey was sure that they could cope, after everything that the last year had thrown at them.

'You're good at maths,' she said as they walked to the school bus. 'And I can always help you out.'

They pushed down to the back of the bus, sitting where nobody could hear them. 'All right, Logic Brain. Work this one out then, as you're so clever,' said Alfie, thrusting a picture into her hand.

It was a pterodactyl. 'Is it PTerror?'

'Nope,' said Alfie. 'It's out of my textbook. We're doing prehistory at the moment. Talk about starting at the beginning. We've got about thirty million years to get to before we even get to anything interesting like war and killing and stuff.'

Janey looked again at the picture. 'So what do we have to work out? It's a pterodactyl, a prehistoric bird like the others.' She lowered her voice. 'Like the sparrow that became the iberomesornis, or the turkey that became the velociraptor.' She found it hard to believe that he could have forgotten so quickly. After all, he wasn't the one whose brain had been blasted by the Spy Film bomb.

Alfie wagged a finger at her. 'Ah, see, that's where you're wrong. It wasn't a bird at all. It was a reptile.'

'No.'

'A flying reptile. Don't you remember? That's what Tish said when she looked it up on the PERSPIRE?' Alfie folded his arms, sitting back rather smugly.

Janey shook her head. 'But that doesn't make sense. What could PTerror have devolved from then? There aren't any flying reptiles today, are there? So it didn't evolve into anything.'

'Exactly.' Alfie screwed up the picture and shoved it back in his bag.

'Well, if it only ever existed at one time, it can't be a current animal or bird so it . . . it had to have come . . . from the past?'

'Right. Well, if you can think of any *sensible* answers by tomorrow morning when this homework's due, SPIV me,' said Alfie, ringing the bell to make the bus stop near Winton School. 'See you tomorrow.'

'Or later,' said Janey suddenly. 'If we have a meeting.'

'What for now?' Alfie rolled his eyes and slumped away down the bus, his sleeves skimming his knees.

And Janey couldn't answer right away. She didn't know for sure, but somewhere in the pit of her stomach her spy instincts were beginning to churn. Where had PTerror come from? The same place her father had gone to when the core of dusky light in the centre of the R-Evolver swallowed him up?

School and homework were going to have to wait – a mission beckoned. Janey waved excitedly to Alfie, but he didn't wave back.

Never mind, she thought. I'll tell him later.

Jane Blonde could hardly wait.

Find out how it all began . . .

Jane Blonde

'Until now, you have been just plain old Janey Brown. But you are going to grow and grow. You will be what your parents have not allowed you to be. It's in your past. And it's in your future. There's a whole new part of you just waiting to you to burst out. You are Jane Blonde – Sensational Spylet. Welcome to our world.'

Follow Jane Blonde on her first non-stop mission!

Jane Blonde
spies trouble

Jane's purr-ecious spy-cat, Trouble, has been kidnapped! A group of mad scientists think they have discovered the secret to a cat's nine lives – but they need Trouble for their experiments. All the clues lead down the drain – spying can be a wet and stinky business! But with chewing gum that lets her breathe underwater, a SPIpod tracking device and a high-speed mini-hoverboard, Jane Blonde is ready for ACTION . . .

Jane Blonde
twice the spylet

Jane Blonde, Sensational Spylet, has just met her secret twin!

When the sisters are posted to an Australian sheep farm, Janey's instincts are on red alert. There's something weird about those sheep. Come to think of it, there's something suspicious about Jane Blonde's twin . . .

Janey can raise an invisible shield with her spy-ring and she can burrow through the earth with her spy-drill boots – but will incredible gadgets save her this time?

Jane Blonde
spylet on ice

Jane Blonde, Sensational Spylet, is hurled on her coolest mission yet when she enrols at SPIcamp!

There are gadgets galore at the top-secret facility and there's even a snowdome where the spylets can chill out. And when the team is sent on a mysterious polar expedition, Janey's spylet-training – and her new snowboard skills! – are put to the test.

Jane Blonde
goldenspy

Janey is delighted when she is granted a dazzling
golden spysuit. But things get deadly serious
when her investigations lead her to a shocking
discovery: her arch enemy has developed a
terrible giant Lay-Z Beam, which he is directing
at Earth from a secret space station! Will the
Goldenspy manage to resist its zapping power
– and save the world?

Look out for Blonde's *last ever* mission!

Jane Blonde
spylets are forever

The past is calling, and Jane Blonde, Sensational Spylet, must travel back in time for her final showdown with the evil Copernicus. But everything works differently here, and she can't rely on her favourite gadgets because spylabs haven't been invented yet!

Coming soon!

A selected list of titles available from Macmillan Children's Books

The prices shown below are correct at the time of going to press. However, Macmillan Publishers reserves the right to show new retail prices on covers, which may differ from those previously advertised.

All Pan Macmillan titles can be ordered from our website, www.panmacmillan.com, or from your local bookshop and are also available by post from:

Bookpost, PO Box 29, Douglas, Isle of Man IM99 1BQ

Credit cards accepted. For details:
Telephone: 01624 677237
Fax: 01624 670923
Email: bookshop@enterprise.net
www.bookpost.co.uk

Free postage and packing in the United Kingdom